HARD LUCK HARRY
IN
DEADTIME

F.A. CORPORAN AND S.E. BRYAN

Black Rose Writing | Texas

ISBN: 978-1-68513-651-2
LIBRARY OF CONGRESS CONTROL NUMBER: 2025934575
PUBLISHED BY BLACK ROSE WRITING
www.blackrosewriting.com

Printed in the United States of America
Suggested Retail Price (SRP) $19.95

Hard Luck Harry in Deadtime is printed in Minion Pro

*As a planet-friendly publisher, Black Rose Writing does its best to eliminate unnecessary waste to reduce paper usage and energy costs, while never compromising the reading experience. As a result, the final word count vs. page count may not meet common expectations.

"For Ana, who taught me to think critically, question everything, and that nirvana was in my head. Thanks, sis."
–F.A. Corporan

"For Tony and Edward, two of the best people I know."
–S.E. Bryan

HARD LUCK HARRY

IN

DEADTIME

CHAPTER 1

"It's only hubris if I fail."
–Julius Caesar

The Hawaiian Islands stretched along the Pacific Ocean in a tidy green line, 6,423 square miles of tropical paradise. The experimental Kāne (Kah-neh) Dark Matter Reactor had been named after the Hawaiian god of creation and the sky. According to a later version of the Kumuhonua legend, Kāne formed three worlds: an upper heaven of the gods, a lower heaven above the earth, and the earth itself as a garden for mankind.

The Kāne Reactor had been built to save that garden.

Nestled on the other side of Oahu, the reactor was miles away from the Ko'olau Mountains, where overrun youth shelters had once swelled with muscular energy into interconnected encampments run by some of the few remaining Kapuna elders. Generations later, under the ministrations of the Reunited Democratic Socialists of America and SOAR IV, along with hefty donations from the DiCaprio Foundation and Harpo Organization, the encampments had long since evolved into a thriving and creative cooperative.

Very few of the Ko'olau Mountains community, however, attended the Kāne Reactor's activation and probably wouldn't have done so even with a gun pointed at their heads. Though nobody actually believed anything would go wrong, they were wise-minded to think *why stand right at the doorway and tempt fate?* Not that forty miles would have helped anyone if something were to go awry. But no one was thinking in those terms, mainly because the alternative was unfathomable.

Everyone remembered that day, the perfection of that day, the crystallized moment featuring utopia's best as streamed and Holo-Cast and pixjumped across the world—the cerulean sky, the quixotic breeze, the arching palms.

Outside of the reactor complex, a small, excited congregation idled together as a single organism. The experimental reactor operated using a thimbleful of exotic matter which had been excruciatingly collected over twenty years. In theory, the reactor could power a large city for fifty years (if the calculations were borne out). The rhapsodic crowd outside inhaled that promise, a heady perfume of hope and optimism, as they counted down from ten to zero in a triumphant roar.

Scientists would later theorize that as the DMR powered up, a micro-fluctuation appeared in the Higgs Field. For the duration of an attosecond, in that specific location, a false vacuum decay weakened the wall between two divergent universes just enough for them to brush against each other. And out of the miscalculation came a microsingularity in the middle of the Pacific Ocean, creating an explosion later estimated at 100,000 megatons.

The fury was elemental and anarchic.

Exaltation abounded one second, terror the next, sliced off mid-cry as the crowds, the arching palms, the mountains, the beaches, the Kapunas' descendants, the hotels, Oahu, and the entire island chain were consumed and incinerated. The Pacific convulsed, vomiting its innards skyward milliseconds before they were vaporized. A titanic mushroom cloud raced thousands of miles in minutes, halfway around the planet, permanently disrupting the rhythm of the Earth.

A chilling dissent sped through the sea, startling billions already wide awake and billions more from their dreams with an eerie, pullulating shriek that some believed poured straight from Heaven. In actuality, as the detonation boiled away immense expanses of the sea and everything in it, the high-pitched keening resulted from molecules being torn asunder and separated into their elementary particles at hypersonic speeds.

The Kāne Reactor, ironically named, annihilated the god's earthly garden in one fell swoop. But the Earth had still been exceedingly lucky that day, because the reaction spent itself almost instantly, and the universe continued on like it hadn't even noticed the blasphemous tinkering of hairless primates.

CHAPTER 2

The People's Republic of Mars (the "Red" Planet)

Winn Sanders could see the dome of Zumba City gleaming from three point two kilometers away. Though his helmet was tinted, he still found himself squinting in the weak Martian sunlight as he gazed across the dunes. *Zumba City, the Jewel of Mars,* he mused, preoccupied. His hands slowly tightened into fists inside his gloves while a low, insistent beeping filled his ears.

Winn tapped his wrist to pop the glitchy readout on, revealing a mild carbon dioxide warning. *Why am I breathing so hard?* he thought, then noticed his fists. With a force of will, he loosened his fingers. *It'll be okay,* he told himself, but his eyes again sought out the city's distant dome, and his thoughts wandered.

The magnificent transparent aluminum dome protected a cluster of medieval-looking high rise buildings and other structures built in the old Zumba crater. The older edifices featured the elaborately scalloped roofs and other familiar flourishes of early Martian architecture. The ability to build high was a point of pride for every Mars-born resident, and renowned Red Planet architect Auxencico Gosse was no exception.

One stately edifice in particular, Gosse's personal testament to the expanded boundaries of low-gravity architecture, was capped by a soaring gilded cathedral spire. Gosse Spire, as it was called, immediately became a popular hangout for the local kids, especially for those who used the apex as a speed gliding leap-off point.

A number of fatalities would follow due to updrafts ripping the daredevils from the intended path down into the park below, instead slamming them into the clear, curved aluminum or spiriting them away straight into other buildings. Security measures added over time to curtail trespassing were all but ignored. Now it was almost a rite of passage to either leap off the spire at the very most, or summit it at the very least.

Winn remembered those days well, since they hadn't been too long ago for him—the gang of kids bypassing security mechanisms, alarms, securely locked doors. The fear and excitement, the muffled laughter, the incredible height, the hammering wind. The view, breathtaking and vast.

Winn had never leaped off Gosse Spire. Something had always gotten in the way—his glider needing repairs, a close friend seriously injured while landing. But that had been years ago, and now he promised himself soon. He'd do it very soon. If things went well today. Maybe even tomorrow . . .

Zumba City, Mars' first settlement, had always been Winn's home. He'd been born there. He knew every street, every alleyway, every brick in every building. He'd never been to Earth and only knew of it from stories he'd heard, along with educational training, of course, on fused quartz crystals, and then old-school photos, video, holos, and related media. When Winn thought of Earth, he thought of two things—how weird it would be to walk around on a planet without a protective suit and helmet. And the Kāne Disaster.

Winn knew about the Kāne Disaster, better known as the Kāne Event, from school but hadn't had to suffer the consequences. He'd heard that many of those who had survived in the rest of the world had come to realize they would have preferred to vanish amidst the heat and light. It would have been quicker and easier than what lay ahead.

Because not only was it *not* the beginning of the end of humanity's perpetual environmental failings, but it was the beginning of something much worse—Earth as a freeze-dried rock where any and every potential resource available and/or yet to be discovered was mined, plucked, planted, skinned, harvested, drilled, deconstructed, and devoured. A purgatorial uphill walk on a down escalator. Except for those who, by fortune of birth, or through long-held relationships with those same, or those with an amassed wealth which could have fed whole countries for decades, of course. Life continued on for them, altered, but much the same, although delays and waiting periods in acquiring desired products and services swelled annoyingly.

The collective eye had slowly swiveled (again) toward Mars. Although terraforming had already been in operation for decades, this had largely been forgotten by the distracted and trying-to-survive masses. Decades earlier, after the SpaceX bankruptcy had sent everyone fleeing and the market plunging dangerously for days on end, all discussion of rockets and space travel and the Red Planet had been dropped from the public eye like a hot potato.

Until the Hawaiian Islands had disappeared and the world had gone cold.

Once interest was renewed in Mars, Winn knew it hadn't looked good in the beginning. The average temperature was an unendurable minus sixty-three degrees Celsius. Wind speeds picked up to twenty-five kilometers per hour in the summer, up to thirty-five in the fall. Scientists labeled the climate unpredictable. Romantics called it whimsical.

It was thought that the oxidization of the soil prevented any biological formation. The lack of oxygen and water combined with intense ultra-violet radiation, dust storms in the south, and severe temps culminated in unacceptable conditions for life.

But, as Winn had learned in school, the decades passed, during which the aggressive terraforming eventually raised the temperature, increased the pressure, and transmuted the deadly atmosphere toward something more hospitable. It was the tip of the iceberg for the future of complete habitation. But something had begun. Mars had been jumpstarted for new life.

In fact, approaching from the depths of space, a visitor would be surprised to observe not the Red Planet but instead a rusty orb with specks of green and a smattering of city lights at the day/night terminator.

Winn had celebrated his twenty-first birthday yesterday. His girlfriend had made him a red cake with a green filling, the colors of the People's Republic of Mars flag—red with its green flower in the middle. Well, almost a cake. It had been dry and tasted strange because of the alternate ingredients used, since the 3D printer needed servicing. But that hadn't mattered. It was the thought that counted.

Which brought Winn's straying thoughts full circle back to today, back to the cloying anxiety he couldn't shake no matter how many times he pictured himself, tomorrow, or more likely in a few more days, leaping off Gosse Spire into the empty air, after all was said and done and things were back to normal here.

Because, as it turns out, Mars was at war.

To the Federal Union back on Earth, the Martians were just squatters. They should not have seceded.

Outside the Zumba City power station, Winn pried his eyes away from the Dome, regulating his breaths, and continued stacking sandbags. He had joined the People's Militia like his father and his grandfather before him so that he could protect their planet, and today they were in full defensive mode. Winn was ready, but he could not control the nostalgia rising in him, a pull toward the familiar, a buffer against the charged atmosphere.

All around the station, militiamen were posted behind perimeter gun emplacements, and others stood at various positions, tensely watching the horizon. Apart from their glass helmets, the bulbous suits of the civilian fighters resembled the Michelin tire man from old-time commercials. They'd been using them for years, unable to afford upgrades. The outside material on all of them was stained red from the sand, and they were grimy and worn. More than a few of the fighters had applied FlexiTape over holes and tears.

The tension in the air twanged Winn's nerves, and he didn't like it. All he knew was that they had been assigned to hold the power station. And he was ready to protect it with his life.

Zumba City, thought Winn with a deep, abiding love. *The Jewel of Mars.*

"Storm's comin' in."

Carl's voice came, low but taut, into Winn's earpiece. Winn stopped stacking mid-action and turned to see a wall of sand like a tsunami racing toward them, edges black and boiling, sparking with lightning. A moment later, a figure appeared from behind a dune.

Winn murmured, almost to himself, "Scout's back."

The scout's transmission stuttered as he approached: *"Th-s-storm! In-side—"*

Suddenly the scout flew forward violently and flopped onto the sand. He sprawled there, unmoving, his back blown open, the rubber of his suit a ruined hole. Winn stumbled back, rigid with dawning.

The storm . . .

He bellowed, *"They're in the storm!"* as a crimson dagger of light pierced the roiling dust.

Seconds before his heart was atomized, images flooded his mind— the endless lanes and channels of the City, sheets of Martian sunlight slashing down, the awesome, unbound beauty of Gosse Spire. He observed the laser forever extending, a spear of amber aimed at him alone, him alone, unwavering, and still the images surged, interspersed with new sensations— a gloved hand sinking into the red Martian soil, the rusty-colored soil giving way, an intense heat like nothing ever felt before, maroon granules twisting in the sun, the red, the red blood bursting from his chest, his mouth, spraying the inside of his helmet, indescribable pain, no time to scream, only time to fall backwards into the russet dust of his beloved planet.

Winn's corpse toppled into Carl who staggered and screamed, "SENTINELS!"

***

First to clear the dust storm, the Sentinel Vanguard Leader rallied forward as satellite transmissions reconnected, streamed through logic circuits, probability matrixes, and topographical map representations of the antimatter reactor—a large containment dome surrounded by a cluster of adobe buildings. It fed vital power to Zumba City. Contour lines snapped into place from multioptics: lidar, infrared, real-time telemetry. A suite of attack protocols were updated and networked across other units.

Vanguard Leader decrypted packets of classified information in nanoseconds. Verify: Secure antimatter reactor. Second verification: Other considerations rescinded.

The militiamen came into sight, terrorists all. They would be eliminated, and the objective would be achieved. The Zumba City Offensive was the last offensive against the People's Militia. Now they would sue for peace. To achieve that end, the Feds released their ultimate weapon, the Sentinels. Cloaked in mystery like legendary demons of wind and fire, if you had the misfortune of seeing one, you were already dead.

Vanguard Leader pierced the distending curtain of dust, slaloming like a skier across the dunes on jet-powered footpads. Behind him, nine other units emerged, each three meters tall, each ten tons of brutal war machine, anthropomorphic, multioptics adjusting, arm-mounted lasers hot and ready.

The nanosecond-long electronic pulses that networked between each machine could be roughly translated into words: *"Engage at will. Vanguard Three, come with me. We will secure the reactor."*

The transmissions manifested to the other units as supreme confidence, perfunctory routine. But these machines would follow Vanguard Leader into hell, or the sands of Mars—take your pick—because myriad other campaigns had known only success, every fighter emerging unscathed.

Vanguard Leader's dissemination of probability trajectories and satellite images of gun emplacements, troop capabilities and site weaknesses were meticulous and ultraprecise, down to weapon strength, design, and functionality from hand held pulse rifles to stationary rail guns.

A pair of mechanized marauders veered from the main group. V Three joined Vanguard Leader while the eight remaining machines sped away, lasers wreaking havoc on gun emplacements as the storm slammed full-force into the structures.

***

Deep within the complex, a shoulder-fired rocket blasted V Five's chest open, sending it crashing through an adobe wall. V Two bulleted past then spun on its jets, flying backwards to pinpoint Five's location before transmitting: *"Vanguard Five—critical damage. Repeat, critical damage."*

"Disregard non-functional units, Vanguard Two. Proceed on mission."

Nanobits of data were logged in Vanguard Leader's file labeled for later inquiry. In a flash, a million permutations of probability filtered through Vanguard Leader's tactical algorithms. How could he have missed a shoulder-fired rocket? The only conclusion he reached every time was: human error. Someone was manipulating the data.

Outside the ruined building, militiamen stood hoarsely cheering until movement within the ragged hole stopped them cold. Recognizing critical damage and following pre-established mission protocols, V Five clawed its way from the rubble, malfunctioning hydraulic joints shrieking. Once upright, it lumbered toward the stunned men.

A synthetic voice placidly announced: *"Critical damage. Self-destruct initiated. Three, two, one."*

The zombie machine collapsed into the emplacement, crushing one fighter, then detonated, taking the scrambling rebels with it.

The rest of the People's Militia were faring just as badly. Black smoke spewed from firefights and skirmishes around the complex, pouring out of obliterated compounds and swirling into the flaying winds, intensifying already-obscured visibility for the rebels and further handicapping their efforts.

Naïve, slaughtered twenty-one-year-old Winn had been horribly wrong to think the skirmish might be over within days. Because the arrival of the Sentinels and the resulting engagement was like a sledgehammer pounding down on a pencil tip, bringing the end much faster than anyone could have possibly imagined.

The Martian soldiers had little or no chance of success.

Deep in the complex, Vanguard Leader and V Three raced side by side, footsteps thundering, decimating resistance en route. At the reactor's entrance, Vanguard Leader provided cover as V Three ripped the panel off the reactor's main hatch controls.

Vanguard Leader glanced over his shoulder. *"Got it?"*

V Three manipulated a bundle of wires. Seconds later, the main hatch opened, and V Three relayed, *"I'm in."*

They hustled through.

Once inside the technology-packed space, the hatch slammed shut. Klaxons wailed and strobes pulsed. The walls were stacked with panels and monitors, rows and rows of switches and valves. The floor had a U-shaped string of workstations jammed with flat screens and coded keyboards.

Vanguard Leader strode forward, laser at the ready, canvassing the room's dark spaces for hidden operators while V Three zeroed in on the main control board. His multioptics scanned turbine and steam generator readings, pressure levels, coolant support and emergency systems.

He transmitted, *"We've got problems. Antimatter containment is collapsing. This place is going supernova in less than three minutes."*

Without warning, every monitor in the reactor room snapped on, filled with the austere image of Colonel Moss. Vanguard Leader scanned the screens wordlessly, even as a molten core that could only be described as dread unfurled within him.

Moss's lean face, dominated by severe cheeks and heavy black eyebrows, radiated authority despite a sheen of sweat shining brightly on his forehead and upper lip. A silver pin gleamed in the shoulder loops of his service uniform beside what looked to Vanguard Leader like the green and red insignia for Mars.

The dread deepened.

As Vanguard Leader and V Three took Moss's image in, a dispassionate statement was broadcast: *"I, Colonel Archibald Moss of Strategic Command, announce my defection and stand with the People's Republic of Mars in their struggle against the tyranny of the Federal Union. At 1500 Martian time, all Sentinel units will be rendered nonfunctional."*

Staggered, Vanguard Leader took one step back.

The units immediately accessed a digital display. Sixty seconds remained until 1500.

The display ticked the seconds down.

Fifty-nine, fifty-eight . . .

Algorithms had been set into motion from the moment of V Five's demise. Tendrils of probability switching on and off thousands of times a second, rendering into an image, into a series of concrete scenarios, presented themselves as one overriding interpretation in Vanguard

Leader's mind. And it disseminated that recognition to V Three. *"It's a trap!"*

. . . two, one.

A pulse of heat and light and radiation consumed all in its path, and the sand and the dirt and debris sucked into the blossoming mushroom cloud burst up and out, painting the surrounding sky black.

CHAPTER 3

There used to be a horn of plenty on Earth called the oceans. Green and white, gold and blue, they lapped near the edges of cities, epic and eternal. Citizens would swing their rods in an arc beneath the shining sun. Fishing boats would cast their nets into the blue heaving furrows of a seemingly endless sea.

Though the oceans were overfished in many areas, most people took it for granted that the sea was simply too big to fail. It would always be there, and it would always provide. On the East Coast, it was true that the sea was still providing. The fishermen still arched their filaments through the air and the boats still tossed their nets into the dark depths. Except there was one big difference—the oceans no longer lapped faithfully at the edges of the cities. The vast waters had receded for countless miles, leaving the craggy, dusty moonscape of the Atlantic shelf behind.

Boats and fishermen swayed on the surface of a still-thriving sea, but now it was 120 miles away, a three or four-hour journey that would have taken, for some, half an hour or less in the old days. The sand was gone. The boardwalk and the piers were gone. The beach was gone.

The apocalyptic surface stretched for miles, clotted with gas and oil rigs which belched fire and smoke like the storied dragons of lore. But dragons they were not. Because the steel jackets and concrete legs would not molder into nothingness like the bones and wings of a biological creature, sinking into the soil, providing fuel for trees and nourishment for the worms. The tubular steel members and sturdy augers of the rigs would persist for decades, nourishing no one, and causing much harm.

The Statue of Liberty stood, bereft, on Liberty Island (formerly Bedloe's and, before that, Love Island) in Upper Empire City Bay, surrounded by nothing but dirt. It perched upon its granite and concrete pedestal amidst the arid soil where attractive landscaping and distinctive trees with plaques proclaiming their species had once grown: little-leaf linden, horse chestnut, Norway maple, Kwanzan cherry, and London plane.

The once-symbolic international garden of dead trees had long been replaced by a new multinational presence—the graffiti of multiple gangs, as represented by their diverse languages: Taiwanese, Mandarin, Nigerian, Tagalog, Czech, English, Mongolian, Russian, and Japanese, to name a few.

There were no tours or water or ferries anymore, but you could still get there. Although you weren't encouraged to. All you had to do was pick your way across the inhospitable surface and sneak past the "road" blocks and a few chain-link fences that were child's play to either climb over or cut through. Which was exactly what the gangs and the homeless and a slew of the wandering lost did like clockwork, regularly visiting the land-locked symbol, not for pleasure but, ironically, for shelter, or to create territorial announcements scripted in black and white or artfully produced in brilliant, elaborate displays.

The cosmopolitan graffiti was only one representation of the major changes that Empire City had undergone in recent decades. In the wake of the Hawaiian disaster which had affected the entire planet, a great migration had occurred. The world's huddled masses had washed up on the new non-shore, bringing with them their languages, religions, spiritual beliefs, cuisine, and customs, and turning the City from a melting pot into a true mosaic.

In an emaciated world, a religion represented by an emaciated Savior simply lost its appeal and gave way to the happier, more well-fed gods of the east. It was a precipitous decline, but when faced with mass starvation, world populations ached for a way off the wheel of incarnation rather than a utopian celestial heaven exclusively for those good enough, earnest enough, or penitent enough to gain admittance. On a dying planet where, at first, every scrap of food required practically a death match to secure, heaven's ticket price seemed a bit out of reach for most.

In the distance, the skyline of Empire City perched on the edge of the dead sea, puncturing the clouds with mile-high monolithic structures. Even Central Park had succumbed to the riot of skyscrapers, its charming rectangle of restrained nature reduced to a peppering of trees existing in the shadow of metal and mortar.

Baxter Parish was old enough to remember some of old Central Park and its former majesty, but he didn't care. As his stretch limo squeezed through the bumper-to-bumper traffic on Broadway, he gazed unseeingly out the window, unmoved by the fact that Times Square, at least as he knew it from media recounts and family stories, was one of the things that had remained more or less the same, although its focus had shifted, settling beneath an Eastern Asian umbrella.

Today Times Square sat shrouded in perpetual twilight at midday, as it had been for the last twenty-five years. Parish's limo crawled forward past the jumble of usual businesses: Kama Sutra Adult Books, The Laughing Roshi's Savings & Loan, Tathagata Florist, and so on, in diverse languages. The Jumbotrons splashed advertising for Third Eye Optometry, Shiva's House of Soy, Dharma Donuts and the latest drive to "Clean Up Lady Liberty." He eyed the crowds with distaste, his gaze skating absently across the teeming bodies.

While the chasm between the haves and have-nots had expanded into a bottomless abyss, people of all classes and professions surged together along the sidewalks and through the intersections of the busiest city on the North American continent. Some of the upper crust activated body shields while in public, something most of the populace could not afford, but everyone still walked shoulder-to-shoulder the same way they had in the past, paying attention to little else but getting to where they had to go.

Used to existing in the perpetual nuclear winter, the crowds were clothed in everything from jeans and cheap plastic jackets to staid business attire to the popular, warm (and expensive) robes made of wool containing an inner layer of sheep fur based on the Tibetan chuba. Knockoffs constructed of polyester fleece were available on every other corner, as were imitations of African dashiki poncho capes, Russian ethnic sarafans, and Greenlandian caribou parkas. Those who couldn't afford fleece or fur or exorbitant leather shoved their hands into pockets made with low quality cotton and synthetic fabrics and pulled their acrylic collars up around their necks.

As his limo stopped beside Eight Fold Path Big and Tall shop, Parish eyed an array of sharp suits in the window, making a mental note to have an assistant return later today and purchase one in every style.

He flicked a switch, rolling his window down to get a better look. The interior of the car was immediately swamped with street noise and complex odors—cooking smoke and grease, rich spices, and sweet-smelling incense.

Along with this also came a band of ragged beggars surging forward and fumbling desperately at his sleeves, including a man wearing a hoodie and tattered coat who, though somewhat hunched over, seemed a lot taller than everyone else. The rest of them, kids and elderly people and everything in between, faces drawn and bodies slight, scrambled for a closer position.

A pair of machine-gun toting bodyguards flanking the car on running boards swung off the limo, preparing to cut the rabble off. Parish tossed several coins into the filmy afternoon light then withdrew, jerking his arm away from the hooded man's especially aggressive fingers.

The guy was big, he noted absently. Healthy looking. He should be out doing construction or something like that instead of shoving starving kids out of the way so he could hustle a few coins. That was the problem with society. Parish had worked all his life. He'd dug ditches, he'd washed cars, and he'd thrown a lotta punches in a crap-ton of bars where he'd gained a reputation as a hard-hearted bouncer. He'd worked his butt off to get to where he was.

The window silently sealed shut. The bank was closed.

Ironically, one of the slogans layered prominently throughout the Square was "Fiske Industries . . . Hard at Work Today for a Better Tomorrow." The beggars, scrambling on all fours to reclaim the scattered coins, would laugh at that and wonder, *When?* For them, the descendants and survivors of the Kāne Event, of Earth getting frozen, of Mars rising as a new hope then Mars lost to Colonel Moss's treachery, "a better tomorrow" never seemed to come. "A better tomorrow" was only a fanciful notion at this point, a child's bedside prayer muttered automatically in the dark.

But today was New Year's Eve and tomorrow would be New Year's Day, the Year of the Rat. A chance to start fresh, renew optimism, begin again . . .

Inside the limo, Parish's worries were light years away from those of the scavengers outside. He reclined in the rear seat and lit a fat cigar with sausage-shaped fingers. His only real concern at the moment was that the cigar hadn't dried out. He had once been handsome, and the ghost of that man still survived somewhere beneath a face like a heavyweight boxer whose prime has come and gone.

Gashes and creases crisscrossed his cheeks like roads that went nowhere while scars pulsed with blood amid puckered skin. One eyebrow had been half-sliced off and his nose had been broken several times, starting when he was eleven years old. He'd never gotten it fixed. Always let it heal on its own. He had been told by many that he snored like a train crash. He didn't care. He didn't trust doctors and never would.

A man appeared on a monitor embedded into the divider and asked, *"Did you hear me, Boss?"*

"I said I'll be there!" Parish yelled at the monitor.

The speaker on the monitor, Preston Marlowe, whipped a thick hank of wavy blood-red hair out of his spectral face, aiming predatory eyes at Parish. As expected, a moment later his hand appeared and combed its way leisurely through the flowing mane. And then again. And then one more time.

"Where you going? Me and English can pick you up if you're running late, Boss."

"I never announce my plans—especially not to you, Marlowe!" Parish snapped off the monitor and yanked the cigar from his mouth, uncorking his irritation, of which there was plenty to share. For one thing, he didn't want that annoying underling Marlowe nagging him. His voice annoyed him, and his hair annoyed him more. He'd never seen a guy touch his own hair so much.

When he'd first met Marlowe five years ago, he'd looked completely different. He'd been bald, had no eyebrows, and his skin was oddly wrinkled, like an unironed sheet. "I got a genetic disorder," had been Marlowe's curt explanation. But an army of specialists, diagnoses, and procedures later, they had slowly pushed that plush thatch from Marlowe's faltering hair follicles and rejuvenated his rumpled skin on top of it.

It was wrong, in Parish's opinion, just wrong. Marlowe had seemed much more feral and menacing when he'd been bald and wrinkled, like one of those hairless cats with the naked, droopy skin, instead of the pretty billboard model he'd turned into. Now all you saw first was the hair; the menace came after, smaller somehow. Pretty didn't get the job done. Parish was a testament to that. And the money! It had cost a pretty penny. A *pretty* penny. Not that any of Fiske's gang had to worry about money, but what kind of a guy spent so much of his pay on his looks?

Parish huffed, shifting in his seat and yanking his shirt straight. He was an old-fashioned guy. *His* buddies spent their Ameros on booze and ladies. And sharp suits displayed in shop windows on Broadway.

He exhaled again, feeling put out. On top of Marlowe irritating him to no end, he also didn't want to go to the boss's estate, because that meant taking an airborne car, an aerolite, and flying made him airsick. So he tried to make his visits to the boss's place few and far between. The thought of flying and getting sick later was putting him in a bad mood, so he decided on a whim that it was time to treat himself.

"The Lotus Blossom!" he yelled at the chauffeur.

Too late. He was already in a bad mood. As the car inched forward, it passed a two-story laughing golden Buddha planted on the island between 7th and Broadway, its arms lifted skyward, smiling beneficently across a scene of mass veneration.

***

As Parish's limo picked up speed, the tattered hooded man on the sidewalk watched it depart then abruptly turned and pushed his way through the swarming streets, passing a group of hooligans surrounding a robot three-card monte hustler.

"Let's go, come on, find the spade," the mechanical hustler chanted. Mostly a dull silver, it had painted a red and black blazer similar to a valet's coat on its upper body and positioned a gray fedora on its head. "Pick the spade, win the cash. It's easy. Even my mother can do it, and she's a vacuum cleaner. Oh!" It emitted a percussive rimshot sound effect.

While it manipulated the cards in a blur, one of the punks tapped the side of his sunglasses and watched through the lenses as the action slowed down dramatically. Catching a move, he abruptly grabbed one of the robot's appendages.

"What gives?" griped the robot.

The thug snapped its wrist back and playing cards spilled out of a slot in the palm. Without hesitation, the hoodlums jumped the rattling machine and began to beat and kick the bolts out of it with steel-reinforced Doc Martins. The fedora flew off and was trampled underfoot.

"Oh. Good shot. That one hurt." The mechanical grifter spoke in a monotone, rolling around on the sidewalk in a parody of pain, and passersby flowed around the scene, never once looking over or breaking stride.

Every inch of the city was crammed with bicycles, cars, motorcycles, rickshaws, tuk-tuks and pedestrians—human, cyborg, and robot. The man in the hoodie dodged a particularly speedy tuk-tuk that had breached the sidewalk, sliding aside with liquid grace as other pedestrians stumbled and fell, cursing the interloper loudly until it slid off the walkway back into traffic.

Sprinting into an alley, the man approached a dumpster. Stained, empty boxes and crates lined the walls and the stink of rotten potatoes and cabbage suffused the narrow space, but the man didn't seem to notice.

He yanked off the ragged hoodie, revealing icy eyes set in an intense face composed of straight, dark eyebrows, a flexing jaw and wide mouth compressed with focus. Long black hair spilled past his shoulders, tied back in a ponytail.

From the dumpster he retrieved and donned body armor, a black duster, and tactical hard knuckle gloves, then strapped a VR visor on his forehead and pushed a transceiver into his ear.

"Link, run the trace."

"Yeah, I'm on it, Harry."

Bending over the dumpster again, Harry straightened up, gripping his Enforcer, a massive four-barreled rifle packing nets, grenades, ordnance and more. Although it weighed around twenty kilos, he slung it across his back as if it was made of paper. Once officially certified, all bounty hunters received an Enforcer from what was left of the Federal Union. Harry had received his many years ago.

A light rustling rose behind him.

A gaunt aesthetic sat lotus-style in a doorway, silently chanting while his fingers moved ceaselessly over his prayer beads. Harry retrieved his ragged coat, removed some coins, and dropped them into the ascetic's begging bowl. The ascetic pressed his hands together and bared a toothless smile.

"The compassionate heart has already attained heaven."

Harry's granite-like countenance remained expressionless as he hurried away.

Emerging from the alley, he blended into the flowing crowd.

Tibetan Monks, dragon dancers, and Hare Krishna revelers tangled together, a frenetic, jumbled hybridization. Kariginu-clad Shinto priests led congregations down the sidewalk chanting the norito past clamoring street vendors selling New Year's Eve paraphernalia along with the usual Hindu god statuettes, the elephant-headed Ganesh most prominent among them.

As he made his way toward the curb, Harry jostled past a robot missing an arm holding a handmade sign that read: WILL WORK FOR RECHARGE. Something almost like resignation rippled across his face, then Harry was blank again, all business, as he ducked into a cab.

A Hanna-hat wearing cabbie shifted in his seat, his mouth wrapped around the tail end of a soydog slopping with ketchup and onions.

"No charged weapons in the cab, buddy. City ordinance."

Wrangling the rifle in front of him, Harry flicked a switch on the butt.

"Where to, pal?"

Harry pulled down his visor and tracked an image displaying a moving green dot and direction.

"West."

The cab began to vibrate with a power-up whine then with a rush of air lifted off.

The vehicle rose evenly past a first layer of traffic and merged with a second layer that crisscrossed the sky in a patchwork of barely organized throngs just as congested as the conveyances on the ground.

CHAPTER 4

The Lotus Blossom Sushi Bar & Teahouse had been operated continuously by the same Bronx family for generations. The original Irish-American-run business had transformed through the decades from restaurant & pub to pub & bordello to dinner theater/night club/underground massage parlor to, finally, sushi bar & teahouse.

Although it presented itself as a traditional geisha house, it was widely known that it combined Western elements along with anything else that made the patrons happy. The present proprietress went by the name of Yoha which meant beautiful, shining autumn leaves, a name she had borrowed from a famous geisha who'd lived in early twentieth-century Japan.

She was fond of donning the formal black kimono and nihongami wigs of a full-fledged geisha, although in her role as an okaasan (mother in Japanese) she really didn't need the wig. Recently, she'd dyed her light brown hair pitch black and, with the aid of extensions, simply styled her own tresses into the traditional poofy upsweep. She had gained quite a bit of weight in recent years and enjoyed the slimming effect the black kimono provided. The drama of the elegant upsweep, she rationalized, drew the eye away from her wobbling chins.

As Parish sauntered into the geisha house flanked by his bodyguards, Yoha appeared out of nowhere and bowed smoothly before him.

"Welcome, Parish Sama. What is your desire?" Yoha inquired with what she believed to be an appealing throaty undertone. She swept her arm outward, completing an artistic half circle, inviting him in.

"I desire stress relief by expert hands. Soothing but eager," Parish answered brusquely. Though far from an elite supermodel himself, the sound of Yoha's hoarse voice and the sight of her Ganesh-sized body made the hair stand up on the back of his neck. He avoided eye contact by gazing with intense interest at his cigar.

"Oh . . . this way, please, Parish Sama." Yoha was pleased with his reaction, feeling that Mr. Parish looked away out of respect for her alluring yet properly restrained sexual allure. She pivoted on oddly tiny feet and began to take mincing steps across the room.

Parish waved a hand at the bodyguards to stay put by the entrance.

Natural light poured in a gray wave from a skylight above a stage where a girl dressed as a maiko, a geisha apprentice, plucked at a samisen, producing a sepulchral melody that hung in the air like smoke. Other maikos engaged a group of gray and black-suited businessmen and one woman before a sushi bar where a cadre of chefs worked with exorbitant steak filets and portions of black sea bass, skipjack, and rare monkfish.

Parish followed Yoha's immense, swaying bottom out of the room and into a corridor with a stairway.

***

Later, after luxuriating in a private bath for a solid twenty minutes, Parish was finally beginning to relax. Yoha entered unobtrusively, pushing the paper fusuma door silently open, and four girls wearing identical robes decorated with various hand-painted phases of the moon filtered in.

"Which one would you like, Parish Sama?" Yoha inquired.

Parish inhaled cigar smoke slowly and devoured the women with his eyes.

"All of them," he grunted in an undertone.

Yoha's eyebrows hitched slightly upward.

"I am beleaguered by stress," Parish added breezily, attempting to veil his naked greed. Then he added gruffly, "I'll take more if they're available," to cover up the fact that he had tried to diminish his greed. Why should he hide? This place screamed greed. He was simply answering the call.

Yoha bowed, declining to address the availability of any extra girls. She ushered the now disrobed, bikini-clad maikos into the bath.

Each bathing suit was decorated with woven lotus blossoms of astounding pink, purple, and magenta hues. The girls giggled and splashed as they vied for position to wash Parish while Yoha neatly folded the gangster's suit and laid it across the bench, unaware of the tiny metal stud attached to its sleeve.

***

One positive had been unexpectedly born from the tragedy of the Kāne Event. At the same time, miles away in the Atacama Desert of Northern Chile, an interferometer detected and recorded massive gravity waves. Once the planet was euphemistically put back together again, the discovery would fuel research into the anti-gravity technology that would revolutionize the world's transportation.

So with very little power consumption, the cab that carried Harry could loiter above the Lotus Blossom all day.

Circling the sky 150 meters above the Lotus Blossom, the cabbie twisted irritably toward the backseat.

"Hey! I can't be hangin' around here all day, pal!"

Without missing a beat, Harry removed a plastic card from his duster and flicked it forward. The cabbie caught it, turned, and swiped it through a meter.

"Yes, I can," he amended, grinning widely. "Yes, I *can.*"

Harry pulled his visor down.

"Link, clear?"

"Yeah. Go for it!"

Harry shoved the gullwing door open. Next, he charged his rifle. Then he threw himself out.

The cabbie leaned out the window and watched Harry plummet downward.

"Now, that you do not see every day."

***

The wind roared in Harry's ears as he dropped like a rock. He pulled in his arms, rifle snug against his chest, and arrowed straight down, duster snapping and thrashing like a giant bat. The building's roof rushed at him, fast. Almost at the last second he aimed his weapon, loosing a barrage of gunfire at the skylight. The glass shattered, raining down onto an empty stage inside.

Harry threw himself back, pulled his feet up, and rocketed past the jagged remains into the building. As he landed, miraculously, impossibly, he tucked and rolled all in one movement, rising lightly to his feet, rifle at the ready.

His voice boomed into the room.

"Federal Regulator. I have a warrant for Baxter Parish!"

Pandemonium erupted as geisha and businesspeople scrambled for the exits. The bodyguards snapped into action, riddling the stage with machine-gun fire. Harry dove and slid across the lounge behind the sushi bar. He flipped onto his back amidst fallen crockery and fish parts, staring up at the cowering sushi chefs who backpedaled and scurried off. He twitched as wood and plaster shards spiked past.

The bodyguards advanced, blasting the bar to bits.

"I'll get the boss!" one of the guards yelled. He galloped toward the rear while the other continued to fire.

"Link."

"Gimme a sec, Harry."

Seconds later, a closed circuit TV image in Harry's visor showed the second bodyguard advancing with machine gun blazing. The trigger clicked, momentarily halting the bullet shower, and he quickly began exchanging clips.

"Get 'im!"

Harry popped up, aimed, and fired.

A net dispersed, whipped around the guard, and snapped him off his feet with terrific force. Bolts pounded into a wall, pinning and immobilizing him. From somewhere above, Harry heard raised male voices. He spun and sprinted toward the back stairway.

Upstairs, the remaining bodyguard crashed through the fusuma door, the delicate paper ripping loudly. Girls screamed and scattered.

"Great Shiva!" Parish shouted.

"We got company, Mr. Parish!" The guard lunged back out through the shredded paper just as Harry turned the corner into the corridor. The passageway was sprayed liberally with bullets and Harry reeled back the way he'd come.

Parish squeezed past the guard, a geisha's ornate moon robe fluttering around his nakedness, and made for the service elevator. The bodyguard followed backwards, keeping Harry pinned down with gunfire until the elevator doors shut.

Harry sprinted toward it.

"Link, shut it down!"

"Can't. It's analog. Didn't think they made those anymore."

Behind him, a door creaked open and Harry swiveled, gun leveled.

Yoha's chins trembled as she took in the massive man, his gun, the ruined, bullet-riddled corridor. It was still said that geisha inhabited a separate reality which they called the karyūkai or "the flower and willow world." Yoha, Irish-American in blood, Japanese in heart and soul, sadly accepted that her delicately constructed karyūkai had torn apart like a paper lantern beneath the violent encroachment of the outside world.

Pressing her palms together before her heart, she bowed slightly in silent acceptance of Yin and Yang as Harry faced the elevator doors. Inserting his fingers between them, he began to pull. Metal creaked and whined, escalating shrilly as he twisted the doors from the frame. Yoha gasped softly at the feat. Once the hole was big enough, Harry hurled himself into the dark shaft.

***

In the elevator cab Parish shot a poisonous look at the bodyguard as the box lowered ponderously.

"Federal Regulator? How'd he get past you two morons?!"

"He fell outta the sky, Boss."

"What?"

A loud thud jolted the elevator, rattling their teeth. Their heads jerked up as the ceiling bulged down.

"Like that, Boss."

"Shoot, you idiot!"

Snapping a transceiver into his ear, the guard let the machine gun rip.

"Pick up on Eighth, now!" he yelled.

Above them, Harry swung away as the bullets turned the elevator roof into Swiss cheese.

"*Sonofa—*" Link's tinny voice barked over the transceiver.

"Link, recon!"

Harry's visor activated. A digital layout of the building rotated, centered, and followed the elevator to the ground floor. The image switched to a closed circuit relay of the elevator door opening and Parish and the bodyguard charging through a fire exit. Several maikos and one of the chefs who had been cowering outside screamed and fled in different directions, along with a startled cat.

Outside, a security camera pivoted, locking on the bodyguard as he crowded Parish back against the building. They huddled between a stack of old folding chairs and a receptacle overflowing with discarded food and hundreds of empty marked-down cartons of the white powder maikos and geishas used to paint their faces. Parish slapped a hand over his nose, glancing down at a half-gnawed fish spine.

"That smell!"

The guard looked around and shrugged.

"It's the alleyway, Boss. It stinks."

They heard the limo coming before they saw it. Out on Eighth Avenue, tires screeched, the horn blasted, and a sanitation-bot lumbered into view. After the bot came the limo which inched past the plodding machine and rounded the alleyway wall. The men bolted toward the car and the bodyguard shoved Parish in and slammed the door. Tires squealed again as the limo peeled down the alley toward the street.

Harry watched them through his visor from the top of the elevator.

"Anything?"

"Yeah, stand by. I got something."

The guard flattened himself against the building, gun cocked, waiting for Harry to exit. The lumbering sanitation-bot suddenly stopped in the street, turned, and blundered into the alley. Extending a pair of pincer arms, it lifted the bodyguard from behind. Reflexively, he compressed the trigger. Bullets soared into the air. The bot dumped the guard into its garbage bin, quickly drawing it closed.

Muffled yelling and pounding immediately followed.

Inside, Harry grabbed the gaping edges created by the gunfire and wrenched the ceiling the rest of the way open. The shriek of rending metal echoed shrilly. He dropped down and tore out of the fire exit. He brushed past the sanitation-bot in the alley, ignoring the bodyguard's faint cries.

Through the limo's rear window, Parish spotted Harry running them down.

"Move this thing!"

"Sir, the traffic's stuck."

"What . . . did . . . you . . . say?" Parish pitched his voice ominously low and let the driver's imagination do the rest. The chauffeur twisted the wheel and gunned it, smashing into a vehicle to his left. The limo mounted the curb where robots and humans dove out of the way as it smashed sidewalk vendors' stands to smithereens.

Exiting the alleyway right after them, Harry spotted the mayhem.

"Link!"

"I'll handle it."

A building under construction swarmed with construction-bots controlled by a hard-hatted foreman seated behind a command console. Ten-foot-tall loader/lifter bots strode around the site retrieving and transporting concrete blocks, girders, and beams with reinforced hydraulic arms and legs.

Suddenly a battered bot carrying a 2,000-pound crate of bricks stopped in its tracks. The crate crashed to the ground, the wood smashing and spilling bricks everywhere. As if possessed, the bot reversed direction and began to trudge toward a fence.

"What the—where you think *you're* goin'?!" The foreman flicked switches, but the bot continued straight through the fence and into the traffic jam.

"I got a runaway!" yelled the foreman into a mike. He spat out the toothpick he'd been chewing on and sprinted for the office and the emergency stop remote.

In the street, the bot barreled through everything in its way, smashing in car doors, denting roofs, and pulverizing a bright blue rickshaw parked at the curb. The limo jumped the sidewalk, veering toward the intersection, and spotted the raging monstrosity too late. The driver's mouth popped open just before a giant metallic claw crushed the hood flat and catapulted him through the windshield.

The trunk jolted open simultaneously. Inside, a stash of weapons glinted in the afternoon gloom.

"Buckle up for safety!" Link yelled through the bot's loudspeaker.

Half a block away, Harry stopped, stunned into immobility.

"Link, I need him alive!"

"He's breathing."

The bot ripped the roof off the limo as Parish rolled out and scrambled back toward the open trunk, the moon robe flapping open and closed suggestively. Grappling with a rocket launcher, he aimed at the machine and fired. Metal and plastic and magnesium alloy burst apart and flew in all directions.

Spinning with an agility born of desperation, Parish located Harry and fired again. Harry leaped sideways as a rocket obliterated a lovingly retrofitted 1959 Chrysler 300, the round headlights looking almost surprised as it somersaulted onto a work van with thunderous percussion. Parish barged through the stalled traffic and backed up on a soydog stand. Peering through the sight, he locked on Harry.

"Sayonara, G-man!" he yelled.

Squeezing between vehicles in the intersection, Harry spotted the rocket flying straight at him. He dropped and slid as it torpedoed past, inches from his head. He felt the breeze. Abruptly, it arced 180 degrees, returning back toward Parish. The soydog vender dove away as Parish and the stand exploded into a million fragments. Soydogs and human meat rained all over the street in unsightly clumps and puddles.

Disheartened, Harry climbed slowly to his feet, taking in the mess.

"Win some, lose some," Link commented lightly.

"Link, stand by . . . "

Harry pawed through the grisly remains, eventually locating an ear.

"Not a total loss."

The longer Harry examined the dismembered body part, the harder reality sank in. He needed more than an ear. He needed more than this. Almost as if in response, his hand began to tremble, and he grabbed it, grimacing.

Not a total loss, he thought grimly. *Not yet.*

CHAPTER 5

The bullet train, crowded with zombie-like commuters along with various deadbeats and ne'er-do-wells, would ordinarily have been a delightful smorgasbord for fifteen-year-old Alexia Eleanor Rosewood. This afternoon, however, she barely noticed anyone and was even too stressed to eavesdrop on conversations, private stories that she would repeat later with comical voices to her best friend Dorcas in their dorm at night.

Right now, after dialing her father's number (for the tenth time), she listened anxiously to the recording on her Holotablet (for the tenth time), willing him to appear. But, disappointingly, the service finished the message, *"Dr. Rosewood is not available to answer your call. Please leave a message. Thank you."* And her father did not interrupt and say, "Alexia, I've been meaning to call!"

Lex threw her head back against the seat in frustration. Monotonous scenery blurred past the windows as the train shot across the empty terrain. An elderly conductor made his way through the tight aisle, scanning ticket cards with a reader. Tamping down her worry, Lex straightened and picked up the Holotab.

She remembered when Dorcas had rushed into their room several years ago, screeching that a new Holotab was coming out soon. She hadn't been as excited as her friend, but the 3D screen with up to 270 degrees of rotation was impressive, and they were always preferable to clumsy VR headgear. Lex smiled, thinking back.

A moment later, grim again, she spoke into the device.

"Dad, it's Lex. I'm coming to find you. I'll be at Grand Central Station in three hours. Meet me if you can, will ya? Love you."

Her mind slipped into the familiar mantra, the recurring mantra of her life: *What have you gotten yourself into this time, Dad? What have you gotten yourself into this time?* She had to willfully make herself stop before she repeated it five hundred times. She brooded as she gazed out the window, the bleak landscape a mirror of her mood.

The conductor appeared at Lex's side looking amused. Preoccupied, she switched the Holotab off, grabbed a teddy bear knapsack from between her feet, and rifled through it. Although fifteen, Lex appeared pre-adolescent with blonde curls bouncing over her blue school blazer and white blouse, which she hadn't taken the time to change out of.

Grinning, the conductor said, "Traveling alone to the big city, are we, little lady?"

Lex handed him the ticket card, narrowing her eyes. She didn't speak for a full ten seconds. The conductor finished scanning in the first three and then spent the next seven losing his grin and waiting for Lex to retrieve her card.

Finally she said, "What's it to ya, perv?" and snatched the card back.

Startled, the old man stammered, "I wasn't—I didn't—"

"I know how to spot a perv, and you look like a perv, perv."

The conductor opened his mouth, closed it, and hastened to the next passenger as Lex grabbed the knapsack and edged down the aisle to the restroom. Inside, she locked the door then turned toward the mirror.

"Dad, what did you get yourself into this time?"

She didn't expect an answer. But it was comforting to say the truth out loud. A possible truth. It would maybe be better if he was just super busy and hadn't found the time to respond to her calls and messages over the past week. Which would be worse, actually, come to think of it, because who did that? People who didn't love you did that.

Don't kid yourself. He loves you. Something's wrong.

And, really, his behavior was nothing new. The epitome of the absentminded professor, Lex pretty much did everything for him. Reminded him where his glasses were. Cooked meals when they were home together. Balanced their finances and remembered to pay her own tuition. Because Mom had died a long time ago, so it was only them. And he needed her because he was badly organized.

Don't kid yourself. Something's wrong.

She sighed and opened the bag.

Removing a small case with a stylus and color palette, she quickly dabbed the palette then touched her blonde hair, instantly turning it jet black. Next she tapped on the stylus, releasing a strong chemical odor, and ran it down the curls until they were bone straight spikes. Then back to the palette with the stylus to blacken her fingernails, lashes, lips, eyebrows, eyes.

"At least you won't look like a total Dwub," she told her reflection. Sighing again, she dumped the rest of her items into the sink beside the palette and stylus. Her Holotab, fortified inside a Rhino case, clattered harmlessly against the metallic surface, along with a cherished Forever-Rose, a package of month-old soy nuts, tissues, and even more revered, her mother's brush, which she never went anywhere without. Then she flipped the teddy bear bag inside out, revealing a skull and crossbones. Relieved to be rid of the teddy bear, the image she presented while at school, she thought of Dorcas, who loved her bag and was always "threatening" to get one exactly like it.

For a girl whose family were adherents of "Silent Jesus," one of the branches of Christianity that the few evangelicals left around the world quietly followed, Dorcas had a dark side to her that Lex was certain her family knew nothing about. Her love of the skull and crossbones bag was just the tip of the iceberg. She wanted to cut school more than attend, she'd gone past second base and had proceeded to (but did not reach) third base with a boy, and she'd even acquired Arctic Pimpanelo Maniac Glass one night and tried to talk Lex into experimenting with the synthetic schedule I narcotic to "unleash their parallel world personalities."

Their boarding school, Flowering Compassion Dharma and Prep School, welcomed all sects and denominations. Dorcas's parents, impressed by the strict curriculum, had applied when Dorcas was nine, leading to Lex and Dorcas becoming best friends and later roommates. Lex's father was a lapsed Methodist, and her mother had been a Pure Land Buddhist. As Lex grew up, he'd venture into spiritual territory whenever she asked (because, as a scientist, he had to be prodded on the subject) but also noticed her interest veered toward Buddhism more often than not. As a result, he began to gently steer Lex in that direction, more than happy to witness the germination of his wife's belief system blossoming in his child.

Upon meeting Dorcas, Lex had been newly reminded of Christian perspectives, like how one could live a life without much compassion for others, be forgiven, and get accepted into eternity without a backward glance. But, as Dorcas often told her, that was heavily frowned upon. Forgiveness should be earned throughout a lifetime, not sought after right at the end.

Though her parents had basically ruined her life by naming her Dorcas (the cry, "It's a Greek name for Tabitha, who was a saint!" from Dorcas always went unheard, and, in fact, only increased the viciousness of the bullying), she was still upbeat and a lot of fun. Lex lifted her Holotab out of the sink and stared at it, contemplating a quick call to her friend to let her know she was okay. Lex hadn't told anyone where she was going.

Forgoing the call until later, Lex scooped everything into the knapsack again and returned to her seat, her thoughts cycling back to her father. If, this time, he had completely forgotten about her, she wondered in that case if he'd be better off with the cause and effect of karma or the fairly guaranteed outcome of his own lapsed route. Lex held her hands out, weighing the pros and cons of each as she admired her fingernails, because there were always pros and cons to almost everything. Her dad had taught her that, and she found it to be true.

The conductor, in the meantime, happened to glance her way and did a double-take. He squinted at her then frowned. Shaking his head almost imperceptivity, he turned and slowly made his way up the aisle.

CHAPTER 6

"There are no rules of architecture for a castle in the clouds."
–Gilbert K. Chesterton

A nameless joy, spurred on by the coming new year, bloomed among the teeming throngs of Empire City, inviting optimism and cheer among even the most downhearted.

Crowds tucked into chicken and fish offerings with excitement and gusto. Some favorite Chinese New Year dishes included an entire chicken to represent unity, a whole fish to signify excess in the upcoming year, and a soft vegetable called fà cài that simulated black hair and symbolized prosperity. There were table upon table and cart upon cart of dried candied lotus root, kumquats, and the sticky and delicious pan-fried cake niángāo. The air was redolent with an exuberance of smells.

On top of the usual tumult, streets clamored with acrobats, opera, comedic skits, dances, and illegal fireworks continuously popping and flashing under the murky sky where loosed red paper lanterns and balloons floated by the hundreds, buffeted by the random explosions.

As a small boy buried his face in a still-warm niángāo, his SmartBalloon slipped from his fingers and took off for parts unknown. The red Year of the Rat balloons featured an animated white cartoon rat and Happy New Year parading across the smart film in white and gold, first in hànzì characters then in English. They were extremely popular.

As the boy gazed after the escaped balloon and started to cry, it was buffeted wildly by street traffic, sending the reactive rat tumbling head over heels onto his back. As it picked up speed and started to steadily climb, the rat jumped up and began galloping, as if running away from the boy and toward freedom, a big grin on his friendly whiskered face.

The SmartBalloon rose and the rat continued to gallop, grinning. Once in a while, it stopped to dance a happy jig, continuing to perform regardless of having no audience. Soaring through the first layer of airborne traffic unscathed, an updraft quickly sucked it up the next fifty meters and deposited it in front of a speeding taxi. The rat ducked in terror and threw its arms over its head. The balloon bounced, unharmed, further up into the sky, pushed this way and that by zooming vehicles, as the cartoon rat cowered and cried huge cartoon tears.

Suddenly, again, the SmartBalloon was free. It entered the clouds and floated for what seemed an eternity in the peaceful quiet. The rat lay beneath the Happy New Year messages alternating above him with his arms behind his head, one leg crossed over the other, the picture of relaxation.

Until the balloon was suddenly yanked upward toward a deep isochronal growl.

Jumping to his feet, the rat shoved his knuckles into his mouth and turned, eyes going comically wide. Gigantic thrumming blades churned like grinding teeth as the balloon was jerked sideways, sucked in, and ripped apart. Red slivers of artificial skin flew out and floated away.

If the skin had still been activated, the rat would have taken in the massive shape sitting several thousand meters above the city—a shatterproof, mist-plated geodesic dome curving massively over a twenty-acre property. The entire area rested on a gargantuan platform kept aloft by six colossal, growling turbines and surrounded by billowy clouds. But the rat was gone and saw nothing. A chunk of balloon with

"Happy" still intact tumbled out of the turbines and continued toward the earth below.

***

Inside the floating property, Solomon Fiske, a corpulent throw-back to nineteenth-century robber barons, stood chipping golf balls in the Great Meadow of his opulent estate. He watched, satisfied, as his last stroke sent the Honma D15 Dynamic Distance ball into a smooth arc, much further than the last one. He relaxed, leaning his tremendous girth on the short iron which bowed slightly under his weight, lost in thought, bathing in the ebbing heat of the spectacular sunset.

Floating above Empire City, above the perpetual cloud cover, all who lived and worked on Fiske's estate were afforded an extra-special perk— the beautiful warmth and light of the sun which rarely pierced the gloom down below.

Fiske stood with his eyes closed in the waning light. His lips were slightly parted and immense jowls sagged off his jaws. His face glistened with sweat that glued the few hairs left on his head to a wide forehead, and every breath he took wheezed softly in and out. His thoughts moved, out of nowhere, as they often did as of late, to his father.

Carmine Fiske had run one of the largest and most successful organized crime syndicates in twenty-first century New York's history. He always made sure to have his pudgy toddler son Solomon, named after the legendary king, perched on his knee behind the massive marble table where he met regularly with his underlings.

In order to keep the child occupied and reduce the expected fidgeting, Carmine would provide the already-overweight boy with a bowl of custard or cookies or gelatins or tarts or mini-pies or pudding or pastries. He made sure the bowl was full to brimming and to change the content every time for an added surprise factor, and he did this for a year of meetings.

One day in one meeting, Carmine's consigliere, Dominic Briggs (Dom to most) rose from his chair, leaned over, and abruptly removed the bowl. Mid-reach for another delicious macaroon filled with a vanilla and almond ganache and finding his hand inexplicably empty with no treat in sight, Solomon was at first stunned and then enraged. As his face turned red and a high-pitched wail poured like a siren from his mouth, all attendees in the room donned headsets, as had been earlier instructed by Carmine. The meeting continued, uninterrupted. Dom had returned to his chair, placed the bowl beside him on the table, and put on his own headset, ignoring the child along with everyone else.

This went on for meeting after meeting for two solid years. Compelled by his father to attend every engagement (except one year when he had the flu and his temperature rose dangerously high), Solomon endured the random psychological torment, screaming and crying and even hammering his father's thighs with his feet whenever Dom took the bowl.

On the days when the advisor didn't remove it, Solomon would hold it possessively against his chest and cram his face as fast as he could with whatever was inside. Over time, the tastes began to meld together, undermined by the expectation of a forthcoming robbery, and the joy of consumption was slowly leached away with Pavlovian relentlessness, although the compulsive eating itself remained.

Although Solomon was very young, Carmine was confident that keeping the boy at the head of the table, steadily absorbing the atmosphere of command and compliance and becoming comfortable, if only subconsciously at first, with delivering mandates that were obeyed without question, would forge an imposing, formidable boss. The bowl experiment would serve to hone in suspicion of others paired with a viciousness inspired by perceived deprivation.

In short: Solomon would learn that what was his was his, not anybody else's, and never should be taken away.

One day two years later when Dom removed the bowl, Solomon didn't cry. The deafening silence that followed the consigliere as he returned to his chair and set down the bowl confused everyone present. Some automatically began to put on the headsets and stopped. Everyone looked around, eyes darting. Should they still put on the headphones? Surely the crying would erupt any minute, having only been delayed. But it never did. Ever again. And on that day, the first day without tears, Solomon sat on his father's lap, eyes ticking alternatively from Dom to the bowl then back to Dom. Glaring.

Years later when Solomon was a teenager, Dominic was found, one afternoon, smothered in a tureen of Lindeth Howe Country House Hotel Pudding. Although Solomon displayed surprise along with everyone else and denied any culpability, it didn't take much imagination to assume who had probably been responsible for the advisor's untimely saccharine passing.

After all, who could ignore the fact that it had been one of Solomon's all-time favorite desserts, a decadent concoction of pudding, caviar, and edible gold leaf? In secret, although there wasn't an ounce of evidence against his son, or even that it had been murder, Carmine was very proud of his progeny. In his eyes, the training he had begun so long ago was complete. The boy who had wailed on his knee was long gone, replaced by the man who knew who he was, what this world had to offer, and just how far he'd go to get it.

Facing the sunset, Fiske's attention was gradually drawn to a golf cart whining its way down a path from a distant Victorian mansion, dispelling his memories. He sighed, not ready for the quiet or his daydreaming to end. The cart's driver, dressed in a butler's uniform, was built like a sumo wrestler, his hair cut in traditional Chonmage style, the vehicle barely able to contain his bulk. As he approached, Fiske suppressed a flare of annoyance at the interruption. *It's not his fault,* he reminded himself. *Mister English is a fine valet. I couldn't ask for better assistance as I run a sprawling city of forty million—maybe more,* he thought with satisfaction.

And it was true. Because Carmine Fiske had done his job well and trained his son with cutthroat diligence. In his teens, Solomon became his father's right arm, and when his father was murdered in his bedroom by an assassin posing as an escort, he took over the entire business without blinking an eye. The murder, however, flooded Solomon with trepidation. Consequently, as soon as he was able, he had the entire Fiske compound reconstructed on a platform, brick for brick, and isolated in the sky.

He also made a conscious decision to abstain from intimate relationships of any kind.

After the debacle on Mars, the destruction of the Sentinels, and the collapse of the Federal Union, what was once organized crime simply morphed into the replacement governments all over the world. Other bosses and warlords took Solomon's lead and constructed compounds on airborne platforms, removing themselves from threat and danger, proving that, in many ways, Solomon turned out to be the model for how to ruthlessly run a territory.

As Mister English pulled up alongside him, Fiske turned and said, "Confucius says a true gentleman makes demands upon himself but not upon others. How true, Mister English. How true."

English waited patiently as Fiske resumed watching the sunset. The silence stretched on and on.

"But I rarely have the opportunity to enjoy such moments," Fiske eventually concluded. He lumbered to the cart and laboriously climbed in.

***

Later in the lavish mansion's grand vestibule, servants descended a sweeping staircase to attend to a light dabbing of Fiske's moist, flushed face with a cool cloth and a change of jacket and fresh ascot. The interior space soared beyond the twelve-foot ceilings of olden days to create steep gabled roofs around which round towers, turrets, and dormers were charmingly placed. The exterior also included elaborate handrails with sawn balusters and intricate corbels spaced beneath several elegant balconies.

Inside, Mister English swept open a pair of doors and saw his boss into a stately meeting hall, the same hall from Fiske's youth, before he turned and left.

There was a humming din of voices. Most of the nefarious underlings situated behind formerly Carmine Fiske's, now Solomon Fiske's, immense marble table took no notice of their surroundings. Fiske, however, breathed in the environment like air, his chest swelling with pride at his father's remarkable taste: the raised panels, voluminous drapes lined with silk, built-in bookcases, and Versailles Castle XVII among the tapestries that lined the walls.

A collection of rare first-edition books, along with most of the tapestries and a Kieninger grandfather clock, had been Solomon Fiske's contribution, a nod to his father's elevated sensibilities. Only two of the tapestries were duplicates. The rest were ancient and authentic. Having been homeschooled, instructed by elite tutors from across the world, there was no mystery behind Fiske's accrued knowledge in many subjects. But he knew he couldn't hold a candle to his father's innate intelligence, a man who had come from nowhere and had nothing, a voracious reader who had been self-taught, motivated by an unyielding curiosity about the world.

Exhaling in satisfaction, Fiske gazed at the wall behind the head of the table, as he always did upon entering the room, where the giant portrait of Carmine Fiske hung, gracing the room with a thoughtful expression. The grandfather clock ticked quietly below. Fiske dipped his chin in a subtle nod of acknowledgement and then turned to the business before him. Bathed in the orange glow of dusk that streamed through an enormous casement window, none noticed Fiske until he said, "Gentlemen, I apologize for the delay."

The chatter faded to scattered murmurs. Then silence.

"I appreciate the rearranging of your schedules for this impromptu gathering." He approached the center of the table, his usual spot.

English returned to the meeting hall followed by several servants pushing an ornate cart laden with cocktails. Rows of crystal glasses clinked musically. Preston Marlowe glided into the main hall wearing a suit that would have kept a family of ten fed for two years and a pair of twenty-four-karat gold-tipped Oxfords that would have paid their rent for a decade. His blood-red hair, the result of the astronomically expensive genetic treatments to cure his alopecia, bounced sumptuously in the breeze of his brisk pace.

Pushing rudely past the cart, Marlowe leaned over to murmur into Fiske's ear. Fiske paused, thinking.

Then: "Presently, Mr. Marlowe. Take the chair."

The room's lush upholstery contained variations of burgundy, ruby red, and plum, and the antique button-back smoking chair Fiske directed Marlowe to was no exception. Though darker palettes had been necessary to hide the fumes released by coal in the old days (and the mansion was heated by solar technology now), Carmine Fiske had had a soft spot for the rich, deeper colors.

Flanked by suits of armor and coats of arms and situated where all could see, apprehensive eyes followed Marlowe as he sank slowly down into the chair as if into a warm bath, soaking luxuriously in its symbolic power. His precious, flowing hair caressed pronounced cheek bones, but he raked his fingers through it only once, too consumed with his sudden good luck to engage in his usual preening. As the guests observed Marlowe occupying the usual spot of Fiske's chief enforcer, they correctly assumed the worst—Parish was either seriously wounded or dead.

"I've invited you here, the Board of Directors, to announce the future of our corporate pursuits." Using a console embedded in the table, Fiske darkened the windows behind him.

"During my reign as Boss of Empire City . . . " He paused and balled his fat hand. "We've squeezed the masses clinging to Fiske Industries' sheltering bosom for food, clothing, water, power—all the essentials of life."

The last of the sun drained away. Accent lights spooled up softly throughout the room.

"As a consequence of our success," Fiske continued, "we've grown stagnant and lethargic." He paused. "It's time to chart a daring new course beyond this eviscerated little world if we're to regain our competitive edge!"

In the ensuing silence, a shriveled, peevish old man leaned forward. The lighting, as gentle as it was, still managed to highlight the bags under his eyes and amplify the creases around his mouth.

"All of our indicators are up. We've invested heavily in recycling technology, at your urging."

Manipulating the table console, Fiske responded, almost tenderly, "Mr. Van Zandt, that was simply a ruse to placate the shareholders while I positioned myself."

Behind him, the darkened windows suddenly came to life with a video display of Mars, and a physical jolt pulsed through the guests.

"I give you Mars!" Fiske finished triumphantly.

Time dragged forward in an uneasy silence. Van Zandt finally broke it.

"Mars is forbidden to off-world commerce. There's a complete embargo. Are you suggesting that we do business with seditionists?"

Fiske turned from the display to grin at the elderly man.

"You misunderstand," he said. Before everyone could finish exhaling in relief, he added, "I demand it!"

Voices rose, unified by a growing alarm.

Unfazed, Fiske gazed around the table, cataloguing their responses. At the sound of Van Zandt's feeble voice again he took in a deep, calming breath.

"It's the only death sentence left on the Federal books," the old man rasped hoarsely.

Fiske reached up to absently adjust his ascot.

"What remains of the Federal Union rents a ten-story building in Omaha, Nebraska. They're hardly a concern." He bestowed a tolerant smile on Van Zandt that was meant for all of them. "No, it's a matter of sheer logistics."

"Logistics?" another voice further down the table joined in.

"Indeed," Fiske said, pivoting to face the speaker. "Necessary for Fiske Industries to become the first interplanetary corporation."

Another shockwave jarred the assembly. Van Zandt stood and pounded the table.

"You're talking treason!"

Silence returned, heavy and absolute. Fiske faced the elderly man.

"Are you . . . tendering your resignation?"

The grandfather clock was ticking from the back of the room, and it became the only sound Van Zandt could hear. *Was it always ticking?* he wondered numbly. He could have sworn it had been dead quiet before. But yet, now . . . tick, tock, tick, tock, tick, tock. . . Swallowing, he glanced around at the others. Their reticent faces were half-cloaked in shadow and the swirling smoke of exorbitant cigars. *Tick, tock, tick, tock, tick . . .*

"Regretfully, I accept," Fiske murmured softly into the smoky room. He turned to his valet. "See that Mr. Van Zandt . . . departs."

Mister English approached Van Zandt who flinched then quickly pulled himself ramrod straight. His resolve faltered only slightly when the muscular servant gripped him by the arm to escort him out. Their footsteps punctuated the stony silence for several seconds after their departure.

"My plan," continued Fiske seamlessly, "requires Promethean vision. The key to our assured success lies in a deal I've struck with an influential contact within the People's Congress." Fiske painted the plan in broad strokes, keeping the finer details to himself. Of course he could never—and would never—fully share, fully explain, fully divulge. But imitating the essence of complete transparency, he retrieved a cocktail from the table where the servants had passed them out, lifted it and finished with, "We're all going to be wealthy beyond dreams of avarice!"

The room erupted into rousing applause. Guests lurched to their feet, delighted with the thought of raising their worth tenfold, delighted with Fiske's galvanizing parlance, delighted with the inspired scheme. Fiske smiled and half bowed with false humility. Marlowe, still seated, smugly raised his glass and smirked. The assemblage began to filter out. Marlowe waited, preoccupied, sipping his cold champagne. Eventually, he reluctantly rose to relay the latest goings-on to his boss.

"It was only a matter of time before Parish's indulgences made him vulnerable," Fiske commented impassively. "Who's responsible?" Fiske faced Marlowe.

"A Federal Regulator. A Mech."

"Bounty hunter?"

Marlowe shrugged.

"We'll deal with it later," Fiske decided. He was feeling upbeat. "What I need now is for you to procure Dr. Rosewood's waning cooperation."

Marlowe nodded, unsure of what "waning" meant. But he had the general idea.

"Since discovering whose DNA he's been working on, the good doctor has become incompliant and needs incentive."

For the millionth time, Marlowe wondered why Fiske didn't just speak regular English but shrugged it off like he always did. He refused to get frustrated right after the triumph of ascending to "the chair" as the boss's number one.

Fiske turned on a Holotab and played Lex's message.

"Welcome Miss Rosewood to my fair city, would you, please, Mr. Marlowe?"

Marlowe plucked the Holotab from Fiske's fingers and grinned wolfishly. *This* was something he understood. Perfectly.

"With pleasure, Boss." he said.

***

Mister English escorted Van Zandt across the great marble expanse of the grand vestibule and down several hallways. Workers either skittered out of the way or nodded deferentially toward the valet, none of which did he seem to notice. The last hallway before they reached the hangar elevator was bathed in buttery yellow light issuing from neatly spaced brass lamps. In the very center of the passage, a framed photo of Moksha dominated the wall, one of her most famous phrases printed in bold gold letters below: "As we are, so it goes."

Van Zandt waited, bristling with irritation and anxiety, while Mister English stopped to straighten the photo (though it wasn't crooked) and to seemingly admire it. A moment later, he abruptly latched onto Van Zandt's elbow once more and ushered him toward the elevator. After walking with the silent valet through what felt like half the mansion, not a word uttered, Van Zandt's nerves were so taut he was seeing flashes in his vision and felt light-headed.

The elevator ride was short. As the bell dinged and the doors opened, Van Zandt faced Mister English decisively.

"Your employer is quite mad, you know." He stared at the valet's profile. "Quite mad."

Mister English's head angled slightly toward the elderly man and Van Zandt held his breath, waiting for the affronted reaction, the outrage. Or would there be a glimmer of acknowledgement, a nod of complicit understanding? In the end there was neither, and Van Zandt counted himself a fool. The oversized valet was a master of his emotions, if indeed he possessed any, and offered nothing beyond a raised arm indicating that Van Zandt should proceed ahead of him out of the elevator.

The valet's silence didn't change the truth, however. Solomon Fiske *was* a madman.

Van Zandt stepped out into the industrial space.

The hangar was a massive enclosure housing parked aerolite limos, a small army of golf carts, a couple of experimental lightcraft in one corner, and other equipment and tech. Workers buzzed in and around it all, accessing computers, control panels and both digitized and old-school charts and maps. Here an army of technicians and mechanics tended to engine and environmental controls on a 24/7-365 basis of rotating schedules. Chauffeurs gathered in loose groups, vaping and smoking while they waited for their clients to return.

Mister English swiftly located Van Zandt's limo and delivered him over to the driver with a brief bow of his head. As the driver opened the door, the older man hissed under his breath, "Let's go. *Quickly.*"

The driver nodded, picking up on the tension, but continued calmly with take-off protocols and preparations.

Mister English watched fixedly as Van Zandt's aerolite glided out of the large open hangar doors. Then he strolled up to the fire control station and activated the image of the departing limo on a console. It curved beneath the twilight sky, heading away into the semi-darkness.

He turned and pressed a big red button, locking a missile on Van Zandt's vehicle.

"Missile away," a computer voice intoned, and a missile rocketed off from beneath the estate.

***

In the limo, Van Zandt, slick with sweat, glanced skittishly out the back window at the receding estate. The vehicle was temperature-controlled and pleasantly cool, but the old man was feverish with dread.

As they continued smoothly on course, a sliver of hope briefly rose within him. After all, he hadn't said anything that wasn't true, even if he was the only one who had been speaking. It wasn't as if he had been threatening. He had only stated what would happen to them all if they pursued Fiske's ridiculous plan.

No. He wanted no part of it. And he was apparently the only one courageous enough to say so. It had been a great relief, also, to put distance between himself and that maniac Marlowe. The man's eyes were as dead as a shark's beneath that absurd blood-red hair, housing no visible humanity. He had sat down in Parish's chair, and that didn't bode well if something had happened to Parish, who was as debauched as they came but seemed like an award-winning humanitarian next to Marlowe.

"How long?" Van Zandt asked the chauffeur, abandoning his useless musings. "We need to get to the ground." His tongue roved through his mouth sluggishly, searching for moisture. *"Now."*

After consulting an instrument, the chauffeur responded, "Ten minutes, sir."

Ten minutes? The sliver of hope evaporated, replaced by a spike of terror which quickly plunged into numb resignation. *It's so quiet,* thought Van Zandt. *And there's no clock ticking.* He felt that this was important somehow. The stillness, the hushed calm, save the muted thrum of engines. It was important. Several moments went by. And then several more. He held on to the feeling for as long as possible.

Then quietly, to himself, almost a whisper: "Alas, oblivion."

Outside, the missile arced out of the sky like a falling star, homed in on the aerolite and detonated, sending it burning and somersaulting through the lowering darkness in a hundred gleaming pieces. In the hanger, English flipped switches, shut down controls, and strolled out without a backward glance.

CHAPTER 7

One Police Plaza loomed starkly in the dusk a mile above the city, police aerolites darting about its Gothic exterior like insects around a hornet's nest.

Harry entered the Federal Law Enforcement office, a tiny, airless space occupied by a stressed middle-aged administrator wearing a rumpled gray pant suit and poring over a computer terminal. A small plaque on the desk read "Milly Pakpao."

Without looking up, Milly raised a hand.

"Just a moment."

A tiny desk fan rotated ironically as a popularized rendition of the old song *Gong Xi Gong Xi* seeped softly from invisible speakers somewhere. The empty walls were unadorned, beige paint lying flat under old-school LEDs. An electron microscope, several empty glass containers, a stack of slides, two lock boxes, and a wrinkled take-out bag from Drunken Master Noodles on Fifth occupied a table beside her.

Rapid-fire keystrokes boomeranged around the small room like automatic gunfire. Every now and then, Milly sighed or shook her head or did both. Eventually, she stopped, hands still poised above the keyboard, and looked at Harry.

"What is it?"

This wasn't her usual department. She was only here this week filling in for Mr. Gao while he underwent a hip replacement that he'd been on a waiting list for for seven years. Harry dropped a baggie containing Parish's ear on the desk. Curious, Milly reached into a drawer beneath the table, located a pair of latex gloves, and efficiently snapped them on. She removed the severed organ from the baggie and slid it under the microscope. Baxter Parish's mug shot appeared on the monitor. Milly's mouth dropped open.

"Baxter Parish?!"

Milly punched information into the terminal, her mouth a gaping hole. The sound of rapid gunfire resumed, echoing around the room.

"It was 50,000 Ameros alive." Milly faced Harry guardedly. "I can only give you 10,000."

Harry placed his PDA device on the desk and Milly quickly entered a stream of numbers to authorize the payment as *Gong Xi Gong Xi* climaxed in the background. Repocketing the PDA, Harry turned and left without a word.

Milly scrambled out of her chair and around the desk, opened the door, and watched Harry until he turned a corner in the hallway. She realized her mouth was still open. She closed it with a snap.

***

Harry sat inside Duesenberg's office, watching as he tipped a plastic cup of milky-looking liquid down his throat. Warm light from a floor lamp flooded the room and spilled out the glass window on the door where Lt. Floyd Duesenberg Cyborg Liaison Officer was stenciled.

"Ahhhhhh." Duesenberg set the empty cup down beside a terminal and a six-inch statue of the elephant god Ganesh holding a bowl. A few beads of the white liquid dotted the neat little moustache that curved down either side of his mouth. He quickly swiped them off then wiped his fingers on an old-fashioned handkerchief.

"Lord Ganesh!" Duesenberg whispered raggedly, pushing the handkerchief back inside his bottle-green tweed jacket. "Harry, you fry your logic circuits?" He leaned forward, his voice strained. "Why not sacrifice yourself over at the Temple of Quetzalcoatl on Chambers? I hear they're short volunteers." He threw himself back in his chair, reached up to adjust his bowtie, also bottle-green, then settled with his hand over his heart.

"Parish killed himself," said Harry. "The rocket was set for heat-seeking."

"Oh, I'm sure that psychopath Preston Marlowe'll take it under advisement after he rips out your hard drive."

"Doesn't this guy ever quit whining?" asked Link.

Duesenberg's stomach rumbled and his hand dropped from his heart to his belly.

"My irritable bowel syndrome," he moaned. "I'll never make retirement with all this stress. It's bad karma. Bad karma all around. My advice, Harry: Get outta town."

"Great. Now he's a travel agent. What next, fortune telling?"

Duesenberg hailed from a family of religiously-oriented activists, lawyers, and even a couple of rogue secular humanists.

Following a near-death experience in his twenties involving a Tibetan street parade and an embittered runaway elephant, however, any musing about abandoning religious dogma like his sister, his aunt, and two uncles had been trampled in the street beneath the bull's feet, along with three robots that had been curious about what a parade was and, unfortunately, the elephant's trainer.

Duesenberg would never forget looking up and watching that giant foot lowering down, so close that he could see the dirt and crust and bits of paper from the street lodged between its toes. It seemed like it had been lowering down for years and years, even as his limbic system took control, breaking his paralysis and flinging his body violently to the left to avoid a towering, stampeding Death by mere inches.

As a consequence, Duesenberg's devotion to his Hindu upbringing tripled, peppered with the inborn pessimism of his personality.

As Duesenberg rubbed his belly and searched through his desk drawers for something, Harry realized his hand was shaking. He covered it with his other hand, concealing the tremor from view.

"If I don't come up with 20,000, you can put me back in the Undertown dump tomorrow," Harry stated impassively.

Rising from the chair, Harry moved toward the door. Duesenberg paused his hectic search, his expression softening. He slid out of his chair and intercepted Harry before he could leave.

"Hasn't Jasper been able to do anything?"

"Does it look like Jasper's been able to do anything?"

"I need the transplant," Harry said, opening the door.

"I'd loan you the money if I had it. I know you're good for it." He reached out and awkwardly patted Harry's arm. Harry gazed at Duesenberg for a long moment.

"Thanks, Floyd. I'll be at Jasper's."

"Sure, Harry. Sure."

The door closed.

Miserable, Duesenberg threw himself back into his chair and dropped some of the milky liquid into Ganesh's bowl, aware, as always, of the irony surrounding his choice of representative deities.

"Life is suffering," he told the round elephant statue glumly.

He received no argument.

CHAPTER 8

A shaft of light pierced the darkness surrounding an empty, decrepit warehouse. A rolling gate activated and rattled open, admitting a semi and trailer waiting outside in the black, black night. A beat-up car, its engine clanking loudly, pulled in beside the truck, and two filthy men, Enzo and Alphonse, jumped out.

Enzo punched a black cowboy hat up an inch off his forehead and rushed to the trailer's back. He muscled a plasma cutter out, ignited it and immediately went to work on the door lock. A third grimy man, Ponzi, with long, tangled hair swinging above his shoulders, shorter than the other two, who themselves were not tall, bounded out of the truck cab with unrestrained excitement.

"We did it, Alphonse!" he crooned with a Texan accent. He did a spontaneous jig on the hard warehouse floor, his little legs twisting and kicking.

Alphonse closed the rolling gate with a crash.

"That's right, little brother, 'cause we followed *my* plan."

Alphonse was the opposite of Ponzi, personality-wise. His hair was cut short and close, military-style, and he wasn't nearly as excitable.

Operating the plasma cutter, cowboy-hat wearing Enzo called over his shoulder, "With these gun parts, maybe we can afford a bath, huh? We're gettin' ripe."

Alphonse bent over, sniffed at Enzo, and recoiled.

"Enzo, I'd say you're way past ripe'n closer to rotten. You stink worse'n Ponzi, and I didn't think that was a possible thing."

Silence reigned as Enzo turned back to the lock and Alphonse moved close to the gate, peering through a tiny cut-out at the dull glow of the moon behind the clouds. He remembered when the moon, and the sun for that matter, had shone freely in the sky, their presence eternal. He'd been a small boy, but he remembered those days, the heat of that orange globe, the brilliance of a full moon lighting up all the dark corners. He sometimes mourned their diminishment, losing himself in memories of happier days.

When Ponzi began hopping in place, Alphonse turned reluctantly from the gate, marshalling his emotions. He'd been taking an Iyengar yoga class recently at the community center in an effort to control his blood pressure, along with his vacillating moods and depression. It was free, as long as you helped put away the mats and the incense once in a while. It was lucky their father was dead and would never find out. If he had, Alphonse was pretty sure his head would have exploded. Then imploded. Then exploded again.

On Tuesdays and Thursdays, the instructors brought in baby yaks to stand on your back. This, too, was free, as long as you helped corral the beasts afterwards. They liked standing on people's backs, but they never wanted to go back into their transport afterwards. Alphonse always turned the yaks down. The thought of hoofmarks on his back made him angry for some reason, so he figured the baby yaks would be undoing all that hard work if he was just lying there, fuming.

No one knew where the instructors had gotten the yaks from. They claimed they had "rescued" them, but from where? Alphonse was pretty sure yaks lived somewhere else in the world, far away from here. He had recently begun to suspect the yoga instructors, Didi and Han, had money, and maybe it was time for him and his brothers to relieve them of some of that money. He just had to come up with a plan . . .

"I wanna buy a burger, Alphonse. I want a real one. Texas style, not one-a them fake meat things."

Alphonse crossed his arms and glowered.

"You dumbass, even if we sold everything in that trailer, we still can't afford no real burger. So shut up!" Closing his eyes, he inhaled and exhaled deeply three times. He pictured a thousand baby yaks standing on top of Ponzi's back.

With a loud crash, the trailer door clattered to the floor. Alphonse shouldered past Enzo, reached in and fished out a Fiske Industries box. Confused, he held it in one hand then pumped it up and down. Something rattled inside.

"Hmm. Lighter'n I guessed . . . "

With Ponzi and Enzo leaning over and practically drooling, Alphonse tore the box open.

"What's this?!"

Alphonse yanked out a small, beige-colored shell-like object.

"A fortune cookie?!"

He hunched over and pawed through the box, tossing out handfuls of fortune cookies with force. They clattered on the floor.

Hushed: "Ponzi, what did you do?"

Ponzi stared down at the box of cookies and scratched his dirty hair. Brows furrowing, he said, "I stole truck three-three seven, just like you said."

Alphonse straightened to his full height of five foot eight, a full inch taller than each brother. He moved in slow motion as if fighting against an invisible, crushing weight.

"Three-three seven?" he whispered. With great restraint, he placed—didn't punt with all his strength across the warehouse—the box of cookies down in the truck. "I said seven three-three. Seven three-three, *lamebrain!*" He stopped, inhaling and exhaling slowly. It wasn't working. "You stole the wrong truck!" he yelled. Enzo reached out to offer a cautioning pat and Alphonse batted the hand away as it was still approaching.

"I ain't no lamebrain, Alphonse," Ponzi whined. "It's my dyslexia. You shouldn't make fun of my handicap. It hurts my feelings."

Alphonse bent forward almost double, his hands on his knees, desperately inhaling and exhaling, only succeeding in making himself dizzy. He tried to remember key elements from his yoga class that aided in control and relaxation, but his mind revealed exactly zilch. Old habits loomed before him seductively, invitingly, and he gave in. He straightened abruptly, grabbed Ponzi by the shoulders, and slammed him against the tool chest. Leaning forward, he pressed his nose against his little brother's. "I'm gonna hurt more than your feelings," he murmured, feeling steam blasting out of his ears, *meathead!*"

Enzo squeezed between them eagerly, holding a fortune aloft.

"Hey!" he enthused. "Hey, it says 'A stranger will soon change your life.'"

As Alphonse opened his mouth to scream at Enzo, the lights went out and a voice boomed over a loudspeaker.

"Federal Regulator. I have a warrant for the Clegg Brothers!"

In the blink of an eye, the brothers scattered like roaches in opposite directions. Ponzi raced to the back of the warehouse toward a rickety-looking staircase and took them two at a time into a wooden loft. Enzo bolted toward the rear of the trailer and climbed up while Alphonse reached behind the tool chest and in one fluid motion retrieved and cocked a shotgun, aiming it sedately.

"Yeah?" he challenged. His blood pressure roared, unchecked, all thoughts of alignment and measured breaths and baby yaks gone, never to return. "Come'n git us, lawman!"

With a thunderous echo, machine-gun fire ripped a hole in the rolling gate. A floodlight splashed across Alphonse as he fired blindly, teeth bared. A whipping sound punched the air. Alphonse was yanked off his feet by a net, jerked backwards, and pinned to the wall. The net compressed his ribs and he could barely breathe, but he hardly noticed.

His bugged-out eyes were glued on the nightmarishly huge figure as it thumped past him, heading for his brothers.

Hiding under a hill of cascading cookies in the trailer, Enzo panted, eyes darting, cowboy hat lost in the sea of hidden fortunes. Suddenly the trailer shuddered violently with a squeal of twisting metal, everything spinning like a dryer, and Enzo scrambled and tumbled in a tidal wave of clattering cookies.

Without hesitation he yelled, "I surrender!"

The tumbling stopped immediately.

Gingerly, Enzo crawled out of the crushed trailer and attempted to stand, stumbling sideways as if drunk. An enormous gloved hand grabbed him and flung him across the warehouse into the back wall. As he slipped into darkness, the last thought he had, staring at the monstrous figure before him was, *"I wish I was drunk."*

As Ponzi listened to his brothers being taken out one by one, he trembled uncontrollably beneath a dusty sheet on a disintegrating, rodent-gnawed mattress. Shifting, his hand sank into something wet and spongy. As the thundering footsteps approached his location, he gagged quietly and whimpered in the back of his throat.

His mind flew back in time, and Ponzi was suddenly eight years old again, trembling in the hall closet along with the family's American Bulldog, Boxer, who'd run in after him, tail wagging, thinking it was a game.

But it was not a game. Ponzi had stolen some of his dad's genuine Texas-made plug—not the synthetic kind—and the sound of boots stomping throughout the old wooden house sounded like a herd of hippos approaching and signaled a beating that even Roy "The Decapitator" Bigolow, Texas's reigning MMA/VFAI champion, would not look forward to.

Right now, though, that beating looked like an afternoon in heaven compared to whatever that thing was that was coming.

The machine gun erupted again in an ear-splitting discharge, followed by the creak of splintering wood, and the loft crashed loudly to the floor. Ponzi rolled out, thrashing under the sheet and yelling wordlessly. After a few seconds of this, he lifted a corner of the sheet, peeked, then popped his head out, his long, disheveled hair covering his face, smiling innocently.

"Oh, hello," said Ponzi from beneath his hair.

The gloved hand reached down deliberately and encompassed Ponzi's face.

***

Stepping easily over all three brothers as they writhed and shouted in a bigger net, the massive shadow bent down and took several leisurely moments to hand-pick a fortune cookie. One crunch decimated the outer shell and revealed the fortune within: *You will reunite with long-lost friends.*

CHAPTER 9

The neighborhood, busy and working-class, bustled with pre and post-dinner hour activity. People alternately strolled and rushed around, engaging in last-minute grocery shopping and errands. Voices, humming engines, and piped-in music created a comforting clamor.

Weaving down a crowded sidewalk, Harry made his way toward a garage crowned by a colorful sign in bold lettering: Jasper's Cyberwerkz Cyber Implants, Upgrades and Repairs. It's AUTOMAGIC!

Harry pressed a button at the front door and waited, absently scanning the street.

"The witch doctor? Really, Harry?" Link was outraged.

A security camera hummed softly as it panned toward Harry.

"Hello?" came a tinny voice.

"Cecil, open up."

"May I help you?"

"I'm here to see Jasper."

There was a short pause. Then: *"He's indisposed at the moment. Please leave a message."*

"What I wouldn't give for a giant fly swatter," hissed Link.

Harry spoke perfunctorily. "Link, access security system and unlock."

Snap, click, pop. The door slid open and Harry entered, passing a scooter parked before a rolling gate near a front office.

Inside, vicenarian Cecil looked like an overgrown spider dropping from the rafters.

Spindly telescoping metal arms and legs whirred and clicked as he moved, covered in beige cargo shorts, a T-shirt featuring a bright sunflower, and a yellow beanie atop a mop of dreadlocks. Compound ocular implants finished off his insectoid look. Every lens focused on Harry as Cecil said, "I routed security through five satellites and seven time zones, and you defeated it like it was nothing!"

"Child's play, termite."

"That's so sterling, man!" Cecil grinned, revealing a mouthful of silver teeth. It was not the prettiest sight ever.

"Jasper?" Harry asked.

"With a client."

Having survived a street-urchin childhood, parents' whereabouts unknown, Cecil had had a fortuitous run-in with Jasper around eleven years old involving Jasper's phone poking alluringly out of his pocket and young Cecil's still-evolving pilfering skills. Jasper had wheeled around and grabbed him by the wrist, removed his phone from the boy's sticky fingers, and the rest was history.

"Come on," said Cecil, motioning with his head.

Cecil had been left in an acrylic Baby Box in the backseat of a taxi, bouncing and bumping around for hours. Unfortunately, it had been a light day for pickups for the driver, on top of which, she'd forgotten to turn on her personal Audio Booster and didn't hear the thin wailing till late afternoon.

There had been a rash of abandoned babies, children, partners, and elderly parents around that time lasting for about five years due to a new drug called Hype flooding the streets which had had a bizarre side effect—users had become convinced that the only purpose in life was to become entrepreneurs. Of any kind. Immediately. Babies were dropped off at hospitals, spouses were abandoned, and eighty-year-old parents were left with cell phones and a gallon of water beside their chairs and beds while sons and daughters and life partners tried to invent a never-before-seen color they planned to market to monks or create a new source of fuel for aerolites out of cacti.

It might have been a miraculous side effect except for the fact that most of the users didn't have the education, means, or resources to tackle the dreams and inventions they suddenly found blooming in their fevered imaginations. And once the fog of faux ambition had passed, nothing had been accomplished for most except that their children had been parceled out to foster care or warrants had been issued for elder abuse.

Cecil had been one of those. He survived Empire City's foster care system until he was nine years old and abruptly decided it was time to make his own way. He ran wild with a gang of kids ranging from younger than him to fifteen, stealing and squatting in abandoned buildings. They eventually discovered the Gracie Mansion Conservatory, which had been bombed thirteen years earlier during some kind of protest, and made their home there for well over two years.

Once with Jasper, it took forever for any sense of security and stability to reappear for Cecil, and it never lasted for long. Even as he got older, the belief that chaos ruled and control was an illusion was overwhelming and debilitating. Only when he had had Jasper remove his frail, soft human limbs and fragile jelly-filled eyes and replace them with unyielding carbon and steel had he felt like he could get out of bed every day, surrounded by armor, and have at least a slightly better chance at not careening, unchecked, back and forth, with no end in sight.

Harry followed Cecil past the front office and the exam room deeper into the garage. The space was populated with an assortment of drills and hammers along with metallic and plastic-molded body parts. There were also several decommissioned domestic robots, one lying on the ground, two standing, limbs positioned as if they were about to walk off, and one sitting upright on a workbench like it was waiting for coffee and its morning news feed.

Cecil clucked his tongue and bent over with his ear near where the robot's mouth would have been.

"What's that, Tinny?" He bent closer then gasped theatrically. "No! We don't got that black market devil juice!"

He grinned his wide, scary grin at Harry and hooked his thumb at the silent robot.

"Illegal oil," he elaborated in a stage whisper, and chortled loudly.

"Where's an exorcist when you need one?" griped Link.

Despite everything, Cecil had a good heart and was upbeat by nature. It was something the Links of the world might not appreciate, but Jasper did.

Cecil and Harry headed toward the back of the garage and the surgery suite, something most people would not expect to see amidst the robot parts and battery chargers. It occupied the last third of the space and the walls and main door leading in were conspicuously white and clean. Inside was a hallway leading to two operating rooms and one recovery room. Storage was laden with gloves, masks, goggles, gowns, shoe covers, blood pressure cuffs, IV bags, electrodes and more.

It was a nice operation and Jasper, the owner, had worked hard to build his business.

The suite's door opened and a punk with a spiky purple Mohawk, covered in tattoos and sporting massive mechanical arms, strutted out, followed by middle-aged, salt-of-the-earth Jasper.

Jasper wore loose dark blue surgeon's scrubs and carried a container sloshing with liquid around a pair of human arms. Known loosely around the community as the FM (Flesh/Metal) Master, Jasper's degrees and certifications in cybernetics and medicine alike made him the most prominent and sought-after FM surgeon for miles around.

Obsessed from a young age by how things worked, Jasper became the go-to person in his neighborhood for any mechanical, digital, or electronic failing. As a young man, he had opened his garage with the intention of focusing mostly on vehicles and electronic equipment. But a parallel fascination with the workings of the human body (along with a pleasant boost in income) led him into medicine and a subsequent marriage of man and machine.

"Not surprised," a favorite uncle of Jasper's used to say. "It runs in the family. What do you expect, being descendants of Lewis Latimer?"

Jasper wasn't a hundred percent certain of his family's claim that they were descended from the nineteenth-century inventor who had patented a unique filament that extended the lifespan of lightbulbs. But since many of Jasper's relatives, close and extended alike, enjoyed lives built on marketing creative, often invaluable ideas, into lucrative and rewarding careers, he wouldn't be surprised.

Jasper stopped walking and held out the large container.

"Hey, kid, your arms."

The punk faced Jasper.

"Toss 'em."

Turning back around, he stepped up to Cecil and slammed his mechanical fist into his mechanical hand with an obnoxious clang.

"Don't need 'em."

The punk eyeballed Cecil. Cecil's lenses whirred and rotated as he stood his ground. Unable to pick an ocular implant to focus on, the punk grunted, shouldered his way past Harry, and stalked out of the garage.

The front door slammed shut.

"Children, can you say Mech-rage?" said Cecil.

Jasper approached a dumpster marked biohazard and tossed the container into it. He turned to Harry and raised an eyebrow. Harry held out his quivering hand.

"It's getting worse," Jasper said bluntly. Cecil leaned forward for a better look.

Harry removed the PDA from his pocket and handed it to Jasper. After reading the display Jasper said, "You're still 20,000 short." He glanced at Harry, not hiding his disappointment. "My guy won't give up the part without we pay in full."

"Why are you listening to this quack? There's nothing wrong with me."

Motioning toward the very back, Jasper said, "Let's have a look at it."

Cecil, way ahead of them, extended his limbs creepily into the rafters and skittered like a spider from beam to beam to the back of the garage.

"Maybe I can tweak it again," Jasper thought out loud, rubbing his chin.

"Harry, the guy's a loon."

They arrived at a space with a metal partition. Cecil was already there beside an MRI machine that sparked and whined when he switched it on.

"Piece of junk!" Cecil groused.

Harry and Jasper entered and stopped cold.

"Behind the shield, Harry!" Jasper barked.

Harry swung behind the metal partition, slipping and falling hard as a strobing flash burst over the top. Rising indignantly, he reentered the machine room and stared daggers at Cecil.

"I'm sorry." If it was possible for a spider to look guilty, Cecil was a master.

Jasper clicked his tongue. "You know he ain't shielded!"

Scratching his head and staring stupidly at the floor, Cecil asked, "Why don't you get a new one?"

Jasper answered with a glare and Cecil clambered back up into the rafters.

"I'll go mind the store."

Jasper faced Harry, hands on his hips, shaking his head.

"Sorry about that." He sighed. "I've trained him in protocol." His head dropped forward. "Where is his brain?"

"Don't worry, Jasper," Harry said quietly.

Still sighing, Jasper motioned for Harry to sit on an examination table. He stepped behind him and loosened his ponytail, revealing a device imbedded into his skull. Jasper attached leads from a computer terminal to it then pulled a rolling stool over and sat in front of the monitor.

"Harry, I don't want this hack messing around inside me."

"Link, stand by."

Numbers scrolled rapidly up the monitor as Jasper punched in data.

"Still making you talk to it?"

Harry nodded.

"I'm putting a tracer on that thing. If it fails, you'll enter safe mode."

"Why's the link malfunctioning?"

Jasper shrugged, reading the monitor. "Artificial intelligence is quirky. AIs can actually go nuts, like people. I'll bet dollars to donuts it's causing your autism."

There was a pause.

"Autism?" Harry asked.

"Yeah," Jasper said over his shoulder, "your lack of emotions. The link is suppressing them for some reason. I know they're in there."

"Maybe I'm just somebody's idea of a bad joke."

Jasper stopped typing and rolled the stool around, regarding Harry sincerely.

"I remember the first day you came through my door all outta whack. I had no idea what you were, but I knew you were unique. One of a kind. Special."

A distant clanging sound issued from somewhere in the garage, followed by Cecil screaming, "CRAP!"

Jasper closed his eyes and sighed.

"Then why was I thrown away?" Harry asked.

A fan clicked and hummed somewhere. Outside, someone honked a horn.

"I don't know," Jasper answered honestly. "What I do know is this link's tied into all your vital functions, including your circulatory pump. We're looking at total shutdown in less than twenty-four hours." He dropped his hands into his lap. "When it dies, you die."

The fan hummed and whirred. Another distant clang sounded, sans screaming this time.

"You have to be alive before you can be dead, Jasper."

Jasper nodded. "Look at it this way. You're constantly processing data in realtime. When the link fails, it'll be the opposite of realtime. It'll be deadtime. Zero processing. Nothing." He rolled back around to face the monitor.

Harry unplugged the leads slowly. "Deadtime," he repeated. "What would that be like?"

Jasper turned and studied Harry for a moment. He leaned back and crossed his arms. "I guess it's sort of like . . . emptiness."

"Emptiness?"

"Yeah. Being one with everything. No object. No subject. Oneness. That's what Buddhists consider enlightenment. Empty mind. No thinking."

Harry looked down at the leads in his hands and frowned.

"Have you attained emptiness, Jasper?"

Jasper laughed and shook his head good-naturedly. "Oh, no, no, no. I'm no Buddha. Not that meditating for thirty years has gotten me any closer to sainthood. Guess enlightenment happens when you least expect it."

Jasper sat looking at Harry with his arms crossed. Smiling warmly, he rolled the stool toward the computer again. Harry continued to frown at his hands.

"Bad karma."

"What?" Jasper said over his shoulder.

"Floyd said it's bad karma. Bad karma all around."

Jasper spun the stool back around. He huffed and rolled his eyes.

"Doozy doesn't know what he's talking about. There's no such thing as *bad* karma."

"If it's not good, it's bad," Harry suggested reasonably.

Jasper looked into Harry's eyes.

"Karma ain't binary, Harry. It's cause and effect. What goes around comes around."

Chiseled face framed by his long hair, Harry gazed back as blankly as a brick wall.

Jasper stood up and shoved his hands into his pockets, gathering his thoughts.

"Okay, once there was this farmer, right?"

"Farmer?"

"Yeah, his mare runs off. His neighbors hear about it and say, 'Oh, what bad karma.' So the farmer responds, 'Good karma, bad karma, whatever.'"

"Oh, I love this story," Cecil said behind Jasper.

Jasper jumped. "Cecil!"

"Sorry." Smiling, Cecil retreated a few steps and stood leaning against the wall. Jasper faced Harry, rolling his eyes.

"Next day, the mare returns with a stallion," he continued, "and the neighbors say, 'What good karma!' The farmer says, 'Good karma, bad karma, whatever.' Then when the farmer's son was putting a shoe on the stallion, it kicks him, breaks his leg. The neighbors hear about it and say..."

"Bad karma," Harry and Cecil said together.

"The next day, a guy shows up to draft the son into the army. The boy's leg is broken, so he's useless and the guy leaves. The neighbors hear about it and say, 'What good karma!'"

Harry's vacant look returned, full force.

Cecil started to say something and Jasper held up a finger. "Ah-buh-buh!"

Cecil closed his mouth.

Harry lowered his visor, deducing that anatomical readings and temperature measurements might contribute to understanding the conversation better.

"See," Jasper continued, "the mare set a series of events in motion that led to the kid not being drafted. Get it?!"

"Yeah!" Cecil shouted as Harry shook his head no.

Jasper turned around slowly and addressed the young adult.

"Do you . . . not have . . . something else . . . to do?"

"Yeah, but I'm not doing it right now."

"Oh, good!" Jasper lit up with fake joy. "Then go do it!"

Cecil's face dropped. Then, whirring and clicking, he obediently exited the room.

Facing Harry once more, Jasper's exasperation softened, shifting minutely. Harry detected surges of oxytocin and vasopressin through his visor, silently connecting their appearance with the small, affectionate smile quirking Jasper's lips.

Turning around that day nine years ago to catch Cecil in the act had led to one of the most surprising joys of Jasper's life—adopting an abandoned boy who had unexpectedly brightened his (unintentionally) spouseless, childless, work-heavy existence with a sweet bonhomie. No amount of money or notoriety or success had ever rivaled the experience of nurturing a neglected soul and having that tender advocacy reflected back with unadulterated warmth and devotion. In truth, turning around that day to find Cecil trying to steal from him had been the best day of Jasper's life.

Jasper sighed and shook his head, but he looked content. "Anyway . . . trust in *your* karma, Harry," he concluded. "Trust that somehow things will work out. Okay?"

The opening twelve notes of the Star Spangled Banner in 8-bit spilled into the room and Jasper handed the PDA back to Harry. On its display, a mug shot of Preston Marlowe and a bounty—Federal fugitive alert, 30,000 Ameros for capture. Location: Grand Central Terminal.

Harry hopped off the table and retied his ponytail.

"What is it?"

"Good karma."

Jasper threw his hands up in defeat. Harry hurried past Cecil who was loitering outside the machine room.

"Link, activate."

"Like I'd actually turn myself off."

"You were listening?"

"To the swami grease monkey? Good karma, bad karma—pah-leez."

Harry was out the door.

"There goes action man!" Cecil said, watching him go.

"Yeah," Jasper commented, finishing up at the monitor, "Give you any ideas?!"

CHAPTER 10

"People who come to New York should enter a palace on the end of their ride and not a shed."
–Real Estate Record and Guide, June 5, 1869

250 years later, the sentiment still thrived, and the grandeur of New York City's Grand Central Terminal remained, despite the kaleidoscope of vendors, performers, and spectators that had transformed it into an oriental bazaar. At its center, a statue of the four-armed, blue-skinned god Vishnu dominated all.

Marlowe and two of his goons, Barry and Vido, wound their way through the bustling crowd past Balinese temple dancers performing before a troupe of musicians. Chiming bells and cymbals and the light percussion of bamboo xylophones permeated the air with lilting notes.

Marlowe paid no attention to the station, its sounds, or its colorful occupants. For some it was simply a throughway, for others it was enchanting. But for him it held only unpleasant childhood memories involving fake blind begging, fortune telling, and tap dancing, all foisted on him by a flamboyant uncle who had had miserable success in the theater.

Oddly, despite the fact that tap dancing was an all-but-forgotten art, people had been fascinated, watching Marlowe as he heel-stepped and shuffled, tossing Ameros at him like there was no tomorrow. The only good memory he had of those times was having smooth, supple cheeks and a head full of his natural hair. Before things had started to go sideways.

"Remember, boys, a simple snatch and grab," Marlowe repeated to the goons, having already given instructions twice before. He realized that he was distracted, busy trying to stuff the bad memories deep down. Especially the fact that it had taken him *forever* to master the single buffalo. He hated coming here.

While unconsciously feeling up his hair with one hand, he nudged Barry with the other. Except it might have been Vido. Marlowe had trouble keeping them straight. He knew they weren't brothers, but they might be cousins. Whatever they were, they looked almost exactly alike. They both had black hair, parted on the left. They were both the same height. They were both muscular in a chunky way.

"It's a kid, after all," Marlowe reminded them.

"Okay, Boss," said probably-Barry, turning away from the dancers he'd been ogling. They were mesmerizing, and Barry was entranced. Dressed in shimmering gold and green costumes including elaborate tasseled headdresses, they alternately stepped softly and stomped while tilting their heads to and fro, their eyes snapping left and right over the top of their hand-held fans.

Marlowe handed probably-Barry a Holotab where he quickly scanned Lex's image then passed it on to maybe-Vido. As they approached the departure/arrival display, Marlowe studied the readout.

"Track eleven."

A gentle notification chime pulsed through the station.

Thanks to the observations of Kingfishers in Japan centuries earlier, the ongoing problem of tunnels and sonic booms had long ago been remedied by imitating the diving bird's streamlined beak. Therefore, the aerodynamic bullet train carrying Lex rolled into the station quietly and without any aural drama.

Marlowe descended the stairs. He snapped his fingers at probably-Barry—yeah, no, definitely Barry, he decided—and pointed to the front of the platform. After jabbing a thumb in the opposite direction, Vido pivoted crisply and headed that way.

The train disgorged a swarm of commuters, and Marlowe swept the platform. Lex appeared out of the horde, slinging the skull and crossbones knapsack over her shoulder, and stood behind him, studying flashing signs. Unaware of each other, they circled back-to-back, turned, faced one another, and leaned sideways past each other to unblock their view. Marlowe pulled his tablet up and studied the girl's face again as Lex jostled past him and hurried up the stairs.

Three seconds ticked by. Then Marlowe's head snapped up. Whistling for the goons, he turned and loped up the stairs after Lex. Catching up to her at the top, he swiftly cut her off.

"Miss Rosewood?"

Lex slowed to a stop as Barry and Vido flanked her.

Smiling slickly, Marlowe said, "Miss Rosewood, your father sent us to pick you up."

Lex eyed the men with unconcealed distrust.

"He did? That's my dad for ya. Never mentioned it."

Marlowe swept his arm out in a genteel manner. "We've got a car outside."

"Okay." Lex took a few steps then slapped her forehead. "I'm so spaced out. He did give you the password, right?"

"Password?"

"You know . . . the password?" Lex waited.

"Of course he did," Marlowe answered readily and pushed his jacket open, revealing a holstered gun. "Abracadabra."

As if choreographed by Bob Fosse's ghost, Barry and Vido swished their jackets open at the same time, paused, let go, and smoothed their individual lapels in tandem.

"Right," said Lex. "That's the one."

All business, Marlowe said flatly, "Let's go, cuddles."

They began walking again, not noticing a security camera panning in their direction. The men casually surrounded Lex. She readjusted her bag, wiped a sweaty palm down her blazer, and covertly looked for a way out.

"Just outta curiosity," Marlowe said conversationally, "what was the password, sweet peas?"

Lex faced Marlowe. One minute she was smiling. The next thing he knew, a shiny black Mary Jane was hurling straight toward his crotch.

"Walnuts!"

The shoe connected solidly with its target.

Marlowe doubled over and Lex darted away. "G-get the girl!" he croaked. Barry and Vido pounded after her.

The platform was empty as Lex reached it, breathing hard. Barry appeared at the far stairwell and slowly moved forward, arms raised to the sides as if corralling a hysterical cat. Spinning around to run in the opposite direction, she spotted Vido strolling toward her. She began to back up the stairs as Marlowe hobbled down, still clutching his scrotum.

"That wasn't very nice, sugar plum." His voice was venomous.

"Sucks to be you right now," shrugged Lex.

As the three of them converged, Marlowe backhanded her, knocking her to the platform.

"Now, we're gonna make nice and get outta here, pumpkin," he seethed.

Lex's hand trembled as she raised it to rub her cheek, too shocked to cry. Marlowe bent, jerking her up roughly, and out of nowhere Harry landed at the bottom of the stairs behind him.

"Federal Regulator."

Marlowe whipped around.

"Preston Marlowe, you're under arrest."

Without missing a beat, Marlowe shouted, "Well?!" at Barry and Vido. He hauled Lex to the platform's edge and jumped down, yanking her with him. Lex screamed.

"Mister, help me!"

Harry slapped the gun out of Barry's hand, simultaneously elbowing Vido then hoisted him up and hurled him at Barry's head.

Marlowe dragged Lex, thrashing and kicking, across the tracks.

"You're gonna get us killed, you bozo!"

"Shut up!"

At the opposite platform, he tossed Lex onto it. As he began to climb up, she grabbed his hair and shoved him back onto the tracks as a net whacked the edge of the platform and dropped, empty, to the ground. Marlowe spotted Harry, on one knee, staring at his rifle, seemingly astounded, then turned back to face the light from a fast-approaching train.

Marlowe yanked Lex's legs from under her and pulled himself up. Spinning her by the arm, he shoved her bodily onto the tracks. She screamed as the train's horn blasted the station. In two bounding leaps, Harry was on her. Gripping her blazer, he leapt onto the platform as the express train barreled past.

A wind vortex surrounded them, sucking at their hair and clothes, and quickly dissipated.

Harry looked up. Marlowe and his goons had vanished.

"The fun never stops."

Though kidnapping, illegal firearms, and attempted murder had most likely not been included in the lofty plans of Grand Central Terminal, Lex nevertheless found herself huddled on all fours, hyperventilating, having almost succumbed to all three.

Throughout the station, travelers continued on their journeys, dancers whirled, and vendors peddled their wares, all steadfastly layering the invisible substrata of their lives around the centerpiece of Vishnu, the embodiment of goodness and mercy, blue limbs shining, the small, knowing smile meant for one and all.

CHAPTER 11

Per the usual routine, the Brazilian cargo ship *Sao Paolo* used the Hohmann transfer orbit to sling around the moon and jettison its cargo into a lunar orbit close enough for tugboats to hoist them to the surface. Her fusion ion engines would then be burned hard for the asteroid belt to pick up the precious ore that every industry on Earth was desperate to get their eager, greedy hands on.

On this route, however, on this particular journey, the aging, battered cargo ship had burned most of its fuel and detoured using a stealthy way back. A round trip of eight months was extended into an extra four. The captain would claim that engine trouble had taken several weeks to correct. He would then also declare that it had become necessary to use the old Mars-Earth transfer orbit, which added additional time.

But what the captain did not report was the extra and extremely armored cargo container that had been attached to the *Sao Paolo* at some point in her journey which housed . . . something other than her usual consignments. And she was returning with more fuel left than could be reasonably accounted for. This was not a problem, for the captain would jettison the extra fuel and limp the last 100,000 kilometers to Earth orbit.

The *Sao Paulo* moved languidly through the inky blackness of space, en route to the desiccated Earth below. Bathed in the dim glow of the instrument lights, the captain and the first officer flipped switches, casually conversing in Portuguese.

Hailing from one of the least populated cities in Brazil, Foz do Iguacu, and raised by schoolteacher parents, the captain had enjoyed an idyllic childhood in the relatively low-crime tourist town. In his teens, before the Kāne Event, he had managed the rubber boat rides where scores of screaming sightseers had succumbed to a drenching from Iguacu Falls, one of the world's largest waterfalls. It was then that he'd realized he would never live a normal life. He required adrenaline, lots of it, along with its requisite catalysts, excitement and risk.

"Incoming message for our passenger," the captain announced.

The first officer punched a series of console buttons. Although the captain liked him, the first officer was his complete opposite, as buttoned-up as they came. But then again, he was from Sao Paulo, a city so crammed full of people that no one had the space to sneeze. The captain had found that without space, without freedom, people became either one thing or another—wild or completely repressed.

"Routing message to his cabin," responded the first officer. "This is a new one, even for you."

The captain slanted him a sideways look. "What do you mean, even for me?"

"Smuggling contraband is one thing. Now we're smuggling people?"

Shrugging dismissively, the caption's teeth flashed in his swarthy face. "If it pays, we haul it."

"Transferring." The first officer spoke into a mike in broken English. "Sir, you have message."

***

The passenger cabin was fit for a king at most. A viscount or unratified lord, at the very least.

Rows of off-white cabinets lined one wall, their pearly nobs gleaming in the low light. A fat recliner upholstered with faux animal skins sank into a thick champagne pile while a king-sized bed sporting a rare Eiderdown throw and cool sateen sheets occupied the center of the space.

The passenger's favorite music, loaded into an audio profile, continuously piped soft, soothing instrumentals leaning heavily toward the cello and muted Dijani bells. A soft blue azurite dressed the walls, completing an atmosphere of tranquil beauty.

In the wall space directly ahead, an imbedded video screen flickered to life and Fiske moved in from the left, his face filling the entire monitor.

"Senator, I pray your journey hasn't been too demanding, and I look forward to seeing you soon. I have arranged for you to be picked up and brought directly to my estate. Welcome home."

The message ended, freezing Fiske's image, his expression somehow simpering and imperious at the same time. An aged hand reached out tremulously and switched off the screen.

CHAPTER 12

At the top of One Police Plaza on the 200th floor, Commissioner Endicott was getting the tongue lashing of his life.

Endicott hailed from an agricultural background, although in recent decades, of course, his family had migrated to 3D food printing, specializing in pizza, purees, and mousses. It was times like these that he wondered if his scorn for sugar-based confectionary had been ill-advised. The clichéd arrogance of youth. Because while dreams of power and prestige might trump those of nozzle extrusions and stainless steel capsules when one was twenty years old, the allure often dissipated in key moments, moments which seemed to have increased at an unpleasant rate in recent years.

And this undoubtedly was one of those times.

As Fiske's bloated, enraged image filled a large video screen and overran its borders, Endicott found himself not only deflating but also cowering, a curious sensation that he did not enjoy. Fiske ranted for what seemed like hours but was probably only seconds, then pulled back, allowing Endicott a glimpse of Marlowe and two of his goons standing in the background, swathed in bandages.

"Mr. Marlowe was escorting the daughter of one of my colleagues when he was attacked by the Mechanoid that abducted her!" Fiske's distorted face returned. Endicott winced. "I pay you to protect the officers of Fiske Industries, Endicott!"

Sweating lightly, Endicott tried to smile. "The city's full of Mechs, sir—"

"I'm talking about a Federal Regulator!" Fiske yelled. "A maniac of a machine with delusions of legitimacy. I want the girl secured!"

The screen abruptly snapped off. Endicott's gaze moved unseeingly toward the window which looked out at Empire City a mile below—the part of it that he could see, that is, between the slabs of upright metal and steel that constituted this concrete jungle. He had been proud of the view once, a long time ago.

Egg on carpaccio and steaming NewMeat paraded out of nowhere before Endicott's eyes, and he wondered idly how his parents were doing. They had never even been up here. *Ah, what did it matter?* he thought. He'd burned that bridge long ago. He slammed his hand down angrily on the intercom button on his desk and shouted, "Bring me whoever's in charge of the Mechs—now!"

***

Duesenberg hyperventilated as he fumbled with the lock on his office door. The bolt clicked into place and he whirled back around to face Harry.

"Preston Marlowe?" He slapped a hand over his mouth, eyes darting. "Preston Marlowe?" he hissed. "Have you flipped out, for Shiva's sake?" He lurched toward his chair unsteadily. "You wanna reincarnate as a toaster?"

"I wasn't born. I won't be reborn," Harry stated calmly from where he sat.

As more holiday music gaily filled the room, Duesenberg bent forward and flicked a switch distractedly, silencing the tinkling bells.

He dropped into his chair as if he weighed a thousand pounds. His bow tie was askew.

"You're conscious, right?"

"Here we go again," Link sniped.

"I process data," Harry answered.

"Same difference. You're a conscious being," Duesenberg said intently. "All conscious beings are on the wheel of Samsara, working off karma. So for compassion's sake, don't kill anybody else." He reached up and cupped his forehead. "I think I have a fever."

Harry pulled down his visor and examined Duesenberg's thermal image.

"You're normal," he stated.

"That's debatable."

Duesenberg appeared marginally relieved. He took a few moments to recoup, then stood.

"The Commissioner doesn't know I exist, and I wanna keep it that way. Quit trying to annihilate Fiske's people, okay?" He was pleading. He approached the door again, hesitated, then unlocked it. He stuck his head out and scanned the hallway skittishly.

"Get to Jasper's and lay low." He started talking faster. "I'll head over there when my shift is up." He paused, tapping his lip. "I might have to work late." He looked at Harry. "No mercy here. New Year's Eve. They don't care." He sighed and closed his eyes briefly. "Hope for some good karma finding that twenty grand."

Harry stood up, nodding wearily, and left. Duesenberg closed and locked the door behind him. Thirty seconds after Harry left, Duesenberg's monitor snapped on. A sultry woman with violet hair, enhanced cheekbones standing out like mountain peaks, and Blitz-shining skin (the latest rage) gazed at him languidly.

"Lieutenant Duesenberg, report to Commissioner Endicott immediately," she intoned in a husky voice.

The monitor snapped off. Duesenberg collapsed into his chair. The joints squeaked. He glared at his little elephant god statue and muttered bitterly, "The deal was I feed you, and you make my life better!"

The statue stared back blankly.

***

A rap on the door preceded his secretary who entered with Duesenberg following timidly. Endicott's eyes razed Ms. Kendall's bright face, bouncy purplish hair coiled around her head, and one-gender-fits-all shiny red Tang suit she'd obviously donned for New Year's Eve, and for a moment it was all worth it.

But then it wasn't.

"What?!" he yelled.

Nerve-wracked, Duesenberg said softly, "Commissioner, you asked for me?"

Endicott stared at Duesenberg, uncomprehending.

"Lieutenant Duesenberg, our Cyborg Liaison Officer," Ms. Kendall supplied in her husky voice.

"We have a Cyborg Liaison Officer?"

Duesenberg shuddered, folding in on himself in slow motion.

"I want the transponder frequency of that Federal Regulator Mech."

"His name's Harry . . . sir," Duesenberg informed him.

"Do I look like I give a damn?!" yelled Endicott.

Another short rap on the door preceded a robust, uniformed SWAT commander. He marched in and saluted, the stiff material of his black uniform bunching tightly around a visibly bulging biceps. Though his buzz cut shone silver at the temples and his face was worn, his body told a different story of amused indifference toward time and the law of gravity as evidenced by the results of his home away from home in the locker room gym.

"Commissioner?"

"There's a hostage situation," began Endicott.

"My boys been itchin' for a little action. Who's the corpse?"

Duesenberg frowned.

"A rogue Mech. What's-his-face here will give you the transponder frequency."

"My name's Duesenberg, sir."

Endicott's head jerked irately in Duesenberg's direction.

"Do I look like I give a damn?!"

CHAPTER 13

The lobby of One Police Plaza was crammed full of people, two seconds away from unmitigated pandemonium, as usual. Perps were dragged in, fistfights broke out randomly, and Tasers were liberally employed amid a babble of voices punctuated by wailing, sobbing, and a few outbursts of singing.

The disheveled denizens of Empire City's overpopulated, crime-ridden streets formed a ragged line before a long wooden desk. *Old Lang Syne* trickled from one hidden speaker somewhere while *Year of the Rat: Xin Nian Kuai Le* banged out of another, engaged in musical battle.

Behind the counter, the desk sergeant, creased face expressionless as he jotted information on a blotter, ignored the yelling drunkard in front of him.

"Izzzzz poliiiiice bru-tal-ity!" slurred the man, staggering in place. He was dressed in a traditional clown outfit, complete with giant purple and yellow shoes and a lopsided orange wig.

"BRU . . . TAL—"

"Next!" yelled the sergeant impatiently.

"BRU—"

"NEXT!" he roared.

The clown recoiled and careened away, making room for Lex who was waiting behind him.

"Yes?" The sergeant did a double-take at Lex's bruised cheek, courtesy of hoofer-turned-gangster Marlowe, but quickly remastered his expression back to its usual poker face.

"Uh . . . I've been trying to find my dad—"

"Missing person's investigation starts with a data search. That's 25,000 Ameros," the sergeant recited with routine boredom. "Provided it turns up a lead, an investigator will evaluate for 40,000 more. If the victim is located alive, there's 100,000 Amero release fee. The judge arranges final disposition for another hundred grand. If the person is deceased, there's a minimum 300,000 morgue fee, autopsy report and final disposition of the remains by cremation or enzyme vat recycling. There's a special on organ extraction. You get ten percent off."

Lex croaked, "I don't have that kinda money!"

The sergeant yanked a stub out of a dispenser and handed it to her.

"Financial aid may be available. Take a seat. Your number will be called for the next hardship caseworker. NEXT!"

A huge person wearing a heavy winter coat jostled past her from behind. Lex shuffled in a daze toward a bench at the back of the room. Squeezing between a woman wearing a pink catsuit and arguing in a deep voice with someone on a Holotab and a man who looked like a homeless lumberjack snoring so loudly it sounded like five rockets launching at once, Lex counted her blessings that at least the drunk clown had disappeared.

Lulled by the station's incessant clamor, Lex nodded off.

A few minutes later, Harry appeared across the room and maneuvered his way through the packed lobby past the desk sergeant.

"But I *have* a permit—"

"Hold it!" The sergeant cut off an elderly lady dressed in military fatigues. Scanning the area, he spotted Lex snoozing with her head on a snoring man's shoulder. "Hey, kid!"

Lex startled awake.

"See that Mech you showed up with tonight?"

"Mech?"

"Black coat. He's an independent contractor. Maybe you could hire him to find your old man."

Blinking sleepily, Lex followed his pointing finger and spotted Harry retrieving his rifle from a security checkpoint. She jumped up, jostling her two bench mates.

"Excuse *you!*" the catsuit lady groused in her bass voice.

The lumberjack's snoring amplified in volume and intensity, as if, subconsciously, he realized five rockets launching wasn't enough and increased it to ten.

As Lex hurried out of the lobby after Harry, the desk sergeant shoved a ticket at the elderly grandma soldier, surreptitiously swiped a tear from his craggy cheek, and bitterly announced, "The end of another lousy year in this lousy town. NEXT!"

Outside in the cool night air, Lex scrambled after Harry. Fireworks popped and whistled, both distantly and close by, and the crush of bodies seemed even thicker than an hour ago. Nudging people out of her way, she watched as Harry slipped nimbly through the crowds, rapidly disappearing.

"Mister! Hey, mister!"

No response. Bobbing and weaving, Lex picked up speed, caught up to Harry, and jumped in front of him, cutting him off.

"Mister, I need your help," she panted. "The cop in there said I could maybe hire you."

Harry stared down at her from what seemed like an immense height.

"I'm not for hire."

He brushed past her and started walking again.

"I gotta find my dad." Lex jogged to keep up. "He's been missing for three weeks. I gotta find him!"

"File a missing persons report." Harry turned a corner and Lex followed.

"Look, mister," she said, puffing, "we haven't got much money, just 20,000, but I'll give you all of it if you help me find my father."

Harry froze.

"I did not see that coming."

A small food server robot walked into Harry's back, bounced off, and clattered to the sidewalk, still managing to keep a packed tray of steaming Bucky coffees upright in one hand. The stream of pedestrians broke around them like water and continued past as the robot righted itself, bowed deeply (coffees *still* intact) and said, "My goodness, I am *so* sorry about that!"

It swiveled and melted into the swarm.

Hands on her hips, Lex craned her head back to see Harry better and pursed her lips, determined.

"So you gonna help me or what?"

CHAPTER 14

Duesenberg trudged back to his office in a black mood, debating whether or not to detour to the break room and plunder the Autocart for snacks. Unbuttoning his suit jacket, he lay a hand tenderly on his stomach and decided not to. If there weren't any plain old potato chips, he wasn't in the mood for frozen coconut meat or chia pudding. He was too stressed out and only had about a teaspoon left of his ginger and aloe soy tonic.

Suddenly the hallway echoed with a deafening thudding that seemed to come from everywhere at once. It sounded like a building had detached and was marching his way. A woman clutching a pile of folders skidded around the corner and hurried past Duesenberg, looking alarmed. Duesenberg turned to watch her then looked back toward the approaching noise. The thumping increased, rattling the glass in the doors. A shadow swept along the wall, rapidly amplifying in breadth and width, as a hulking silhouette approached.

A gargantuan cowboy wearing a leather duster and ten-gallon hat rounded the corner dragging the netted Clegg brothers behind him.

"Leonard?" said Duesenberg, gaping. "Leonard Little?"

"I don't go by that name no more, Doozy," the giant flared indignantly. "It's Colt. Winchester Colt," he said in a deep bass voice.

Duesenberg forced a smile, treading lightly.

"Well, it's been a while, huh?"

On the floor, two of the brothers—Alphonse and Enzo—writhed and struggled, muttering, limbs hopelessly entwined. Ponzi lay unmoving, as if dead.

"Five years," answered Winchester.

Duesenberg gestured toward the motionless man.

"That guy okay . . . ?"

"He's asleep." Winchester didn't even look. "I'll register with you after I hand these boys off to the Feds."

Hearing Winchester, Alphonse and Enzo twisted around to get a better look at Ponzi. Enzo poked him and Ponzi expelled a loud burst of flatulence. Ignoring all of this, Winchester lumbered forward.

"Have you run into Harry?" asked Duesenberg.

"Naw. Just got back in town." Winchester kept walking.

"Well, Len—uh, Winchester," Duesenberg said impulsively, "if you owe him a favor, right now would be an excellent time to return it."

Winchester stopped and turned, staring at Duesenberg with an unreadable expression.

"A favor?"

As the conscious Clegg brothers resumed their fruitless thrashing, he absently tightened his grip on the net and slowly pushed up his ten-gallon hat. *"Igne natura renovator integra,"* he rumbled. He paused for dramatic effect. "Sure. I can do that. Things are different now."

Duesenberg nodded emphatically. *That* was an understatement.

"Igne natura renovator integra," Winchester repeated, in case Duesenberg hadn't heard it the first time. "I learned that from one of the most brilliant, craziest bounties me and Harry ever did together." He smirked. "A beautiful Egyptian gal that liked speakin' Latin."

Without another word, he turned and lumbered away as Duesenberg nodded and murmured, "Through fire, nature is reborn whole."

***

Seven years ago...
The hacker was world-renowned and had a bounty to match. And there was double jeopardy to boot: the quantum computer used to decipher encrypted data.

Harry and his trainee Leonard Little stood outside a hermetically sealed building in New Brooklyn studying a gigantic black metal structure lacking windows or any visible entrances.

"The whole frigging center's a faraday cage," Link informed Harry. *"Electromagnetic fields completely blocked. Impossible to hack. Gutsy."* Link paused. *"They also have no idea we're out here. Works in both directions."*

"Yeah," Harry responded. "Their procedure's pretty water-tight, too."

JJ the hacker, known only by one name, like legendary Elvis, or the more recent, grandiose Moksha, made a living by deciphering the encrypted information of Western bloc data centers, information worth untold amounts of money. Couriers delivered the data that needed to be decrypted, JJ cracked it, then bodyguards delivered the hard drive by hand back to the client. Only *after* payment did JJ furnish the password that would release the de-encrypted data.

Leonard, standing at five foot, one inch, stared up at Harry restlessly. What he lacked in height he made up with zeal and no small amount of swagger.

"How're we doin' this?" A deep voice rolled paradoxically out of his diminutive person. He gestured emphatically. "No doors." He angled his head toward the metal building. "Blow a hole?" He made a face. "Or cut one. Use the torch. Less detectable."

Link sighed. *"Hold on. See those steel slabs set at intervals? Like they're just part of the construction? One of 'em's a door."*

When Harry didn't answer, Leonard rolled his eyes impatiently behind a pair of military-style goggles, turned, and scampered toward the corner of the building. Harry craned his head back, scanning the gargantuan wall.

"There it is. Thirty meters to your left. One-meter thick. Steel reinforced concrete hatch. Hatch door wheel on the inside."

Harry approached the spot.

"Ahhhh. Place started as a hideout for one of those powerful families fleeing Luxor back in the day. JJ's a descendent. Full name's Jamila Jaafari. Lots of security reinforcements and measures already in place before the faraday renovation."

"How does that help us?" asked Harry, absently watching as Leonard returned from jogging around the building. Now he brandished his Persuader, a handgun loaded only with stun darts. As a trainee, he wouldn't receive the federally assigned Enforcer until he'd passed probation and became a certified bounty hunter. He walked up, panting lightly, and said something.

"It doesn't help us," Link continued. *"Faraday's somewhere in the middle—way in there. But there's a way in and out. Waste processing system. Stand by for schematic."*

"Knock, knock!" Leonard said, pulling Harry's attention away from Link. "Okaaaaaaaaay." He hefted his weapon aggressively. "Like I said, what's the plan?"

***

The grate was on the east side of the structure, camouflaged behind a series of hedges landscaped to resemble what looked like the three main pyramids of Giza in Egypt. Visor down, Harry bent over the grill.

"Carbon steel. Tensile strength, 580 Moa. Chromium woven through."

"Really?" Leonard snorted, kneeling down. "They add vibranium or adamantium while they were at it?"

"Napoleon Bonapart's got a point."

"At least it's not tungsten," Harry noted.

He removed a carbide-tipped blade from somewhere on his person and went to work on the four corners of the grill. Once done, he inserted his gloved fingers and heaved backwards. The tortured metal complained then abruptly snapped off.

"So much for all that," Leonard nodded toward the massive, ostensibly impenetrable building. He fiddled with his weapons belt, searching for explosives, then downsized again to the plasma cutter, then glanced back at the exposed hole and said, "What now?"

"*Ha,*" Link said humorlessly. "*Put it together, Yuri Gagarin.*"

"Link . . . " Harry said on a long, simulated exhale produced by an air diaphragm in his chest connected to his voice box.

"*What? I'm doing him a favor. Gagarin was five feet, two inches!*"

Facing Leonard, Harry paused. He nodded toward the small, gaping space. He raised his arms to the side and made a show of scanning the considerable width and height of his entire body, then dropped his arms. He stared at Leonard meaningfully. Leonard's eyes ticked between Harry and the hole, the hole and Harry. Then suddenly it clicked.

"Oh, no. No, no, no, no, no, no." Leonard's eyes blazed from behind his goggles. "NO WAY."

***

JJ's familial hideaway had been expanded over the years until it became like a mini-Egyptian dynasty of its own. Beneath, various processing channels split in different directions, leading to at least five different buildings clustered in the protected core 500 meters away. Once Harry got Leonard through one of the chutes and inside the complex proper, the cage would take over and all communication would cease.

By the time Leonard slogged through the filtration system's tunnels, secured entrance and then doubled back, using hasty calculations along with guesswork to ballpark the direction of the front door, fifty-five minutes had gone by, and Leonard was traumatized for life. He and his weaponry were covered by a hair-raising sludge that smelled like a thousand rotting bodies along with bits of foodstuff, greasy, disintegrating paper, and other unidentifiable pieces of trash.

As his oil-slickened hands slipped on the hatch's door wheel over and over, he finally ripped off his gloves, threw himself on the wheel, and wrenched it around with his entire bodyweight. The door punched inward, shoving him back into the wall, and Harry stepped through quickly, charging his Enforcer. An alarm immediately began blaring.

"Thanks. Let's go."

"I think I saw something, Harry." Leonard clawed at Harry, gripping his duster as he strode by. His face was haunted. "Something living down there."

"Get a grip, Tiny."

"Come on, this way." Harry shrugged Leonard off and stalked off.

"It had lots of legs," Leonard shouted. His voice broke. "It had *hands!*"

Scooping his contaminated gloves up and stuffing them away, Leonard shadowed Harry down a hallway covered ceiling to floor with bas reliefs of ancient Egyptian palaces depicting beautiful courtyards framed by tamarisk trees, surrounded by gardens with fish ponds and fig trees and intricately tiled swimming pools shaded by date palms. Noticing none of this, Harry plowed forward, dropping members of the security force as they popped up from around corners and out of the woodwork. Leonard struggled to regain his composure and control of his oil-slickened equipment.

"Room on the left, fifteen meters ahead," said Link.

"This way," said Harry, stepping over a prone, stunned guard.

He kicked in a door, revealing a medium-sized room drowning in more Egyptian-themed art. The walls shone with bright reds and yellows and greens overlaid with depictions of ancient rulers—Khufu, Ramesses II, Hatshepsut—and interspersed with a plethora of gods from famous Osiris to lesser known Geb.

As four guards with I'M WITH PHARAOH emblazoned on each of their beige and gold faux armored shirts/leather skirts rushed them, Harry zoomed in on the back of the room.

In the back, JJ spun around, eyes wide in a caramel-colored face.

Dressed in a yellow wrapped linen skirt with a red and white double crown on her head proclaiming PHAROAH, she whirled back toward an intricate machine made of looping, interconnected silver and gold pipes and blinking lights and began typing rapidly on a keyboard beside it.

The stone wall behind the quantum computer was dominated by a bas relief of Imhotep, resident chancellor of the Third Dynasty of the Old Kingdom and the world's first documented multigenius. Black bold letters emblazoned in the wall just above his skullcap proclaimed: KNOW THYSELF.

Fumbling with his equipment, Leonard struggled to engage his Persuader as a blur of linened death surged toward him. Reeling backwards, he fired and watched as the darted bodyguard continued forward for three or four steps then dropped onto his face.

Leonard gained his feet, staggering as Harry bounced off him. Stunning the next guard, Harry charged forward, ducked beneath a viciously arcing machete, and tasered the attacker on his vulnerable neck. He quickly pumped the Enforcer, releasing a net that wrenched the last man sideways off his feet, pinning him to the wall.

"Imhotep is the gods' work!" JJ screamed across the room, frizzy dark brown locks tumbling from beneath her towering crown. An axe had somehow appeared in her hands, and she swung it upward over the quantum machine. "But I'll be the one who ends it!"

"She means the machine!" Leonard yelled. "Imhotep's the computer!"

Grabbing Leonard by the vest, Harry hurled him bodily across the room. He slid like a skeet ball straight into JJ's legs. JJ flew backwards and the axe popped out of her hands. The double crown of Lower and Upper Egypt spun off and came to rest against the wall beneath a panel depicting the Eye of Horus, a stylized black and white representation that seemed to be watching everyone.

"Bet they woulda used bullets if they knew she was gonna wreck the thing anyway."

"Yeah. Lucky for us," Harry acknowledged. He bent to help Leonard up then moved to secure the bounty.

"*Sic semper tyrannis!*" JJ shouted out of nowhere from the floor as Harry pulled her arms behind her sedately.

"'*Thus always to tyrants,*'" translated Link. "*You got it backwards, lady. You're the tyrant.*"

"*Igne natura renovator integra,*" JJ continued cryptically, her eyes flashing first at Harry then at Leonard. "I will go on! This is but the cleansing fire of rebirth—Uggggggghhhhhh!" she moaned, interrupting herself as Harry helped her to her feet. "WHAT IS THAT SMELL?!"

Leonard had discovered part of a burrito lodged in the seam of his vest and yanked it off angrily. Glaring, he lunged forward. Harry stopped him with one arm.

"You tell ME," he yelled. "It's *your trash,* lady!" He then switched focus to Harry, simmering with barely-contained rage and humiliation, seeing himself being tossed across the room over and over. Harry had gone too far this time. Harry had crossed the line.

As a probationary bounty hunter, Leonard would only receive a fraction of the payout. Therefore, later, when Duesenberg sniffed the air, covered his nose and almost threw up, Leonard seriously questioned whether any of this was even worth it.

CHAPTER 15

" . . . and so I left the boarding school. He's absentminded sometimes, being a scientist and all, but he's never been outta contact this long." *He has not forgotten about me,* thought Lex. *He has not.* With a force of will, she shoved her doubts away and gave them a healthy kick for good measure. "You listening?" she asked after receiving only silence as a response.

"Give it a break, kid," groused Link.

Lex and Harry were hurrying down a bustling sidewalk toward Harry's apartment building. Or Harry was striding normally, and Lex was struggling to keep up.

Stopping abruptly, Harry turned and trotted up the front steps of an old tenement building.

"When are we going to look for him?"

Lex put her hands on her hips, chest heaving, and watched Harry disappear inside the building. After a moment, she quickly followed.

Harry was already double-stepping it up a dark stairwell that had seen better days. There was a strange chemical smell in the air like burned circuits. Lex jogged after him, gasping. On the next level up a door opened and a small, hooded figure the size of a child came out lugging a trash bag in its arms. Smoke billowed in the air around it as it set the bag down.

"Hi, Harry!" the figure said in a friendly, feminine voice.

Lex realized it wasn't a child. She stopped walking and stared.

Without altering his stride Harry called back blandly, "Ann."

The figure looked at Lex as tendrils of smoke wound into the air from beneath a bright blue dress topped with a white apron. It pushed its hood back, revealing a short-circuiting Raggedy Ann-bot.

"Hey," Harry's voice came from above somewhere. "Come on."

Lex walked away backwards, mesmerized.

"Hi!" said Raggedy Ann. "Hi! I'm Ann!" It lugged the bag behind it toward a garbage chute in the wall, wobbling unevenly. Metallic items in the bag clanked and clattered as it was dragged along the floor. "Parts," it said, and shrugged at Lex cheerfully. "Nothing works, though!" It opened the chute, lifted the bag, and pushed it inside in slow motion. Then it giggled and waved its hand through the smoke. "I'm so sorry you had to see that!"

With a burst of energy, Lex sprinted up the last of the stairs to the top where she bent over, gasping, as Harry unlocked his door.

"Wow . . . no . . . elevator," she wheezed. "How . . . retro."

A series of loud clacks punctured the air and the door popped open. Harry walked in and Lex followed, entering a small studio apartment consisting of a kitchenette (empty and pristine), a brown sofa made of an unidentifiable material, a large armored locker against one wall, and a terminal resting on a modest coffee table. She made a beeline for the sofa and collapsed. It was relatively quiet in the room, the street noise from below fairly muffled. Even the random pop of fireworks seemed far away.

"Cozy," she said, looking around. "I'm Lex, by the way. Lex Rosewood."

"Harry." He set down his rifle.

Lex spotted a framed photo on the table and picked it up. In it Harry stood with a small man, maybe five feet tall, dressed like Harry and holding an Enforcer, trying to look tough.

"Who's the guy in the picture?"

"My ex-partner, Leonard Little."

Lex looked back at the photo and smirked. "That's sort of on the nose," she said under her breath. She rose distractedly and wandered toward the window. "You have . . . interesting neighbors."

Harry bent over to switch on the terminal. He looked like he wanted to sigh but he didn't.

Cecil's face appeared on the monitor.

"Jasper's Cyberwerkz—oh, hey, Harry."

"Jasper."

"Sure thing." Cecil's implants rotated, fixing on Lex. "Hel-lo!" His mouth stretched into a shiny, flirtatious grin.

"Eew. Not even," Lex scoffed.

Undeterred, Cecil asked, "Who's the lovely lady, Harry?"

"Jasper!"

"Sheev! Cool your jets, Ace."

Cecil quickly clicked his tongue at Lex before the image switched to a gigantic pair of eyes. Lex flinched. Jasper flipped up a pair of jeweler's glasses.

"Harry?"

"I've got the rest of it."

"That's great!" Jasper was excited. "Transfer it."

Pulling her Holotab out of her bag, Lex hooked it up to the terminal and called up her account information.

A muffled chorus of voices laughed then burst into song in the distance.

"Got it," said Jasper. "I'll send Cecil to get the part," he continued briskly, "but I want you here, Harry, where I can monitor you."

"I'm on a job. I'll get to the shop as soon as I can."

Nodding reluctantly Jasper said, "Just don't knock your head around. That thing's on its last legs, and we're cuttin' it real close." Jasper looked right and left. "Cecil!" he yelled. "Where are you? Pick up! The directions are uploaded."

Cecil's distant voice responded, "Can I take the van?"

"No, you can't take the van. You'll make much better time on the scooter."

"C'mon!" Cecil whined off-screen. "I hate the scooter! After my last upgrade, my legs are too long for the pedals. My knees'll be in my armpits and I'll probably crash."

Lex glanced at Harry who stood watching Jasper who was listening to Cecil complain. They heard footsteps approaching onscreen. Jasper's eyes narrowed dangerously. "Cecil …"

"Okay, yeah, they'll telescope up. I can make 'em fit!" Cecil leaned into view with a pained expression. "But it's uncomfortable for long periods of time!"

"Cecil … "

Cecil threw out one hand. "Okay! Okay! Where to this time?" Jasper handed him the Holotab and there was a pause as Cecil scanned the directions. Then, aghast: "HOBOKEN?!"

Jasper closed his eyes. A light chime, and they were both gone.

"You're making a big mistake, Harry. I'm fine."

Harry removed his duster and body armor, laying them on the back of the sofa. Entering the kitchenette, he removed a pillbox from a cupboard and drew tap water into a glass as Lex invaded his privacy by pulling open the coffee table drawers and snooping inside.

Finding nothing of interest, she slumped, sighing.

"Hey, I'm starving. You got anything to eat around here?"

Harry approached with the water and a small capsule. Lex perked up.

"Wait a minute. What are you, some kinda pervert?"

"Swallow it."

"Nuh-uh."

"It's a tracking capsule. I can locate you if we get separated."

Lex stared at the pill as if she had x-ray eyes, which she didn't. "Is it radioactive? I mean, like will it give me brain damage?"

"Too late, kid. You can't unscramble eggs."

"It's inert. It'll go through your digestive system in forty-eight hours."

He shoved the glass and capsule in her face. Pushing herself back into the sofa didn't help, because the glass and pill followed.

"Swallow it."

Lex sensed no room for argument on this. Unhappily, she snatched the capsule and drank it down with a gulp of water.

"Where was your father's last known location?" Harry asked, returning to the kitchenette. "And what business did he have with Preston Marlowe?" He opened the refrigerator and removed a small aluminum canister as Lex wandered over.

"Uh . . . Sutton Towers, suite 702. And I have no idea what that psycho's got to do with him."

She ran her finger along the compact counter and inspected it, impressed. "This place is spotless." She glanced around. "My dad's a total S-L-O-B."

Harry lifted his shirt and pushed against his abdomen. An access panel slid open and he switched out an identical canister for the new one.

Lex stared, stunned.

"Holy Sheev!" She watched as Harry set the spent canister aside and tucked in his shirt. "I thought that cop was, like, joking. You're a robot?!"

"Give the kid a prize."

"I thought you were dreamy, but you just put the kibosh on that." She pressed a finger to her temple and blinked. "Dee-leet."

Harry stared down at her. "I'm an android, not a robot."

"What's the difference?"

"A robot's an appliance. I'm self-aware."

Lex nodded. Then she muttered under her breath, "Guh. Superiority complex much?" She hugged herself and ogled him. Harry ignored her as he opened the fridge again. Retrieving another canister, he poured it into a glass and handed it to Lex.

"If you're hungry, drink that."

"What is it?" She held the glass up and squinted at it.

"Harry . . ."

"Synthetic proteins with a polymer lubricant. It's safe for humans."

Lex handed the glass back to him. "No thanks. I'm trying to cut down."

Harry exhaled and set the glass aside.

Link's urgency ticked up a notch. *"Harry!"*

A voice boomed out of nowhere through a bullhorn. *"Mech, come out, or we'll blast you into spare parts!"*

Rushing to one of the only two windows in the room, Harry stayed to the side and peered down. The SWAT commander stood below, one foot casually propped up on an armored Ryson LION fender, directing activity near armored personnel vehicles as a SWAT tactical unit stormed the building.

"You've got one minute, Mech!"

All at once a stupefying variety of robots clattered out of the building and crashed through windows to the sidewalk with their arms raised in surrender. The SWAT commander face-palmed.

"The Mech *holding the female hostage come out*," he clarified into the bullhorn, "or we'll blast you into spare parts!"

Inside the building, the Breach Unit approached Harry's apartment utilizing standard tactical maneuvers. On the floor below Harry's, the glitching Raggedy Ann-bot opened its door to investigate the noise. Swirling smoke preceded it into the hallway.

"Hello?" Raggedy Ann called in a bright voice.

The screaming of conflicting orders began immediately.

"Hands up! Hands up! Hands up!"

"Get on the ground!"

"Don't move! Don't move!"

"Drop! Drop down! Get down!"

Startled, Raggedy Ann started to raise its arms, then switched direction and put its hands on its hips.

"Which one is it? Make up your mind," it told them sternly.

The cops let loose. A salvo of bullets slammed into the bot, spinning it around, decimating its blue dress and frilly apron, the stuffing flying out of it in poofy bundles. It fell onto its side facing the wall, its voice stuck in a friendly loop. "Hello! I'm Raggedy Ann. Can I come over and be your friend? We can have adventures together! Hello! I'm Raggedy Ann . . . "

On the top floor, a tech cop scuttled to Harry's door, accessed a panel, and hooked up an electronic device.

In the apartment Harry said, "Link, shutters."

Steel shutters dropped over the windows, clanking and locking into place.

"What's going on? Who're you talking to?" Lex glanced around, confused.

"They're trying to override my security protocols."

Harry retrieved his body armor, coat, and visor from the back of the sofa and quickly dressed. Crossing the room in three steps, he removed ammunition from the armored locker, reloaded his rifle, and stuffed his vest's catch pockets.

"What kind of scientist is your father?"

"A geneticist."

"Time to school ya."

As the tech cop outside the door finished punching numbers into the electronic device, the panel strobed with high voltage, humming shrilly. The cop was blown backward into the Breach Unit, scattering them like bowling pins.

"Amateur."

Standing in the center of the living room, Harry removed a cylinder from his vest.

"Find cover!"

Lex dove behind the kitchen counter as Harry straight-armed the cylinder onto the ceiling. It attached and exploded, showering them with dust and debris. Lex rose in degrees, taking in the gaping hole. She stepped around the counter.

"I don't think you're getting your deposit back—"

Lex was suddenly flying straight up through the hole. She landed on her side on the rooftop, dodging her knapsack as it sailed up after her.

Pounding thuds issued from below before the door gave with an ear-splitting crack. Officers charged forward, firing blindly.

Lex scuttled backwards as Harry vaulted effortlessly through the hole, barely pausing to tuck her under one arm before racing across the rooftop under the black night sky. Lowering his visor and running the night vision Harry said, "Link, escape route."

"East. Next building. Fire escape."

"Who-are-you-talking-to?" Lex grunted as Harry ran.

Cradling Lex in both arms, Harry hurdled an alley, a floodlight illuminating them like day, and landed lightly on the roof next door. The roofline immediately ricocheted with bullets.

"Cease fire!" yelled the SWAT commander in the unit's coms. *"Bring in the air units!"*

Harry shielded Lex's head as the rain of bullets swelled then subsided.

Wrangling herself loose, she shoved at him roughly, stinging her palms in the process.

"Quit Mech handling me!"

Her eyes widened as a bright light flooded the roof. Harry swerved seamlessly, pulling her toward a fire escape ladder, as an aerolite mini-van swooped in, cutting them off. Harry swung his Enforcer up. A gullwing door arced open and a voice called, "Harry, get in!"

CHAPTER 16

Lowering his weapon slightly, Harry peered into the aerolite's dark innards.

"Come on, Harry, move it!"

Harry pushed Lex's shoulder and hurried her toward the vehicle as low-flying spotlights loomed in the distance. Inside, he secured her in the back then lowered himself into the passenger seat. The aerolite lifted up and Lex turned, staring out the window. The pursuers looked far away. She exhaled and slumped as Harry briefly studied the driver's face.

"Leonard Little?"

Winchester reached over and poked Harry's chest.

"It's Colt now. Winchester Colt. That name don't apply no more, for obvious reasons," the hulking cyborg informed him.

"Snippy much?" said Lex and Link simultaneously.

The vehicle flew steadily through the night as Harry and Winchester stared ahead out the window, not speaking. The silence was awkward and heavy.

"Friend of yours?" asked Lex when she couldn't take it anymore. She hated awkward silences.

"Me and Harry go way back," Winchester responded.

"Weren't you in Texas?" Harry asked.

"Trailed a bounty here," his former partner answered coolly. "But I'm thinkin' 'bout stickin' 'round. Can ya handle the competition, me all Mech'd out an' all?" Winchester's teeth flashed in the darkness.

"That's your decision." Harry watched the traffic flow past his window in a river of light.

"Still a charmer, eh, Harry?" Winchester said, then laughed.

"Still a jerk, eh, Leonard?" murmured Link in Harry's ear.

The aerolite quickly gained altitude and swung into denser traffic. The heavy silence had returned and taken up permanent residence. Winchester steered the vehicle nonchalantly with one arm until he looked into the rearview mirror and stiffened. Lex turned to peer out the back again, alarmed to see pursuing air units gaining on them fast.

Quickly, Winchester snapped on the radio and pressed transmit.

"Traffic Control, this is Federal Regulator A1521-214 requesting Tier 1 access. A1521-214. Tier 1 access. "

Static filled the car then a voice said, *"Affirmative, A1521-214. This is Traffic Control. Priority Tier 1 access granted. Good hunting."* Three layers of airborne traffic in Empire City started a hundred meters up with workaday vehicles like trucks and slow heavy transports occupying the first layer. Fifty meters above that was normal everyday traffic—cabs, limos, commuters. The last layer, fifty meters above everyone else, wasn't free. This was occupied by those with cash to spend, along with government and emergency vehicles. The last layer enjoyed the privilege of more isolated space, like the HOV lanes of the past, and guidance control. Limiters kept the first two layers restricted to their levels.

Immediately Winchester altered course, flying straight up through to layer one, passing by trucks and cabs and limos. His navigation lights speared the darkness. Both he and Lex looked down and watched what seemed like a fleet of pursuing units scream by in the lower tier. Casual once again, Winchester placed his arm back on the wheel and relaxed in his seat. It creaked loudly when he shifted, as if it was about to collapse or possibly disintegrate. Harry went back to staring out the windshield again and Lex did the same out her window.

"Where you need droppin'?" Winchester asked.

Lex unbuckled herself and leaned forward, thrusting her face between them.

"Sutton Towers, suite 702," she told Winchester. He flashed her an annoyed look. Then he snickered.

"New partner, Harry?"

"Client."

"Hmm." Winchester sucked his teeth. "Going private, huh? Business slow?"

When Harry didn't answer, Winchester shook his head and Lex sat back. The aerolite banked smoothly to the left and merged through midtown and the continuing spectacle of New Year's Eve festivities. Lex flattened her face against the door window, taking in the bursting fireworks, bouncing balloons, and jubilant revelers. She could not believe the size of the crowd in Times Square, a number that seemed to swell well past the 50,000 who had attended the Tabango Bay concert in D.C.'s Herzog/Brown Arena two years ago.

Lex pressed closer to the window, flooded with memories of the day that she and Dorcas, thirteen at the time, learned that the Filipino boy band Tabango Bay would be touring in their city. Well, Dorcas had found out, because she'd been a die-hard fan since age eleven, and she had photos of every single member—Crisanto, Rizal, Danilo, Xavier, Benigno, and of course Enrique Corazon, hidden in her underwear drawer and secreted beneath her mattress. She had even acquired, at one point, Enrique Corazon's (supposed) pamphlet of love poems online and kept a copy stuffed inside her school blouse for at least a month until the discomfort forced her to settle for propping it up in their tiny, shared bookcase.

Lex did not understand Dorcas' obsession at all. She thought the whole boy band thing was immature and silly. But after listening to Dorcas cry every day and every night for a week straight that her parents would never let her see a Tabango Bay concert, and they could never afford it anyway, Lex decided to take action. She swore to her up and down that not only were they going to see this concert, but she'd get them in for free. Because that's the kind of thing friends did for one another.

Dorcas remained inconsolable, convinced that Lex was studying too hard and her mind had slipped into a fantasy world where everybody's dreams came true. So when the night arrived that Lex snatched her Holotab out of her hand, interrupting a viewing of Tabango Bay's year-old interview with Mr. D., the Godfather of Sufi-hōgaku fusion, yanked her off her bed and said, "Let's go," Dorcas thought they were just going to raid the kitchen for custard again.

But they were not raiding the kitchen for custard.

The next thing Dorcas knew, they were sneaking off campus, running like thieves through dark streets, squealing and grabbing each other when somebody yelled, "Hey!" from a parked car, and hurtling down the stairs into the dangerous, night-time subway. Ten uneventful stops later, they arrived at the Herzog/Brown Arena. At the entrance, Lex began working her grifter's magic with a story of parents trying to park in the jam-packed lot but urging she and Dorcas on ahead so they wouldn't miss a single song.

The ticket taker, who was not buying the spiel on any level, was about to tell the girls to step back when screaming and yelling erupted to their immediate right. The second his head turned, Lex and Dorcas were under the turnstile and scampering at light speed into the arena's interior. Shouts of, "Hey! Come back here!" rang out after them, duly noted but categorically ignored. As the friends squeezed, shoved, and crawled their way past a wall of hysterical, screaming teenaged girls, the dulcet tones of the Pinoy boy band stroked Dorcas' ears and caught Lex's growing attention with a touching cover of Menudos' "Cuando Pasara" in Tagalog.

They arrived at the stage just as Enrique Corazon, the love of Dorcas' life, took the mic. His heavenly ink-black mane tumbled alluringly over one eye while the other eye zeroed in on Lex and Dorcas, still panting from their twenty-minute ordeal to get to the front of the crowd. Then he gestured for them to join him.

Dorcas's brain short-circuited and her eyes rolled up, dropping her in a dead faint. Moments later, Lex left her in the capable hands of the concert medics while she was lifted onto the stage by a pair of beefy security guards. Enrique circled her like a roving panther, serenading her with the band's third hit, "Suborbital Flight To My Heart" in a Tagalog/English mix. As he enchanted her with his suave vocals and soulful brown eyes, Lex had no idea what was happening to her. Her entire body went numb, she couldn't tear her gaze away from his no matter how hard she tried, and she was barely able to lift a hand to receive the Forever-Rose he presented to her at the end of the song.

The arena erupted into thundering applause and screams of joy as everyone at the concert, including the 300 million worldwide telepresence, took in the flamboyant gesture, a symbol of the band's catch-phrase: "The Philippines may be gone, but Pinoy love lives on."

Among those who had been watching the streaming, Holo-Cast, broadcast, and pixjumped concert were several students back at Lex and Dorcas's dorm, huddled furtively over their tablets. Unable to contain their excitement over two of their own not only making a successful end run to the Arena, but one of them standing on stage, mere inches away from Benigno, Rizal, Xavier, Danilo, Crisanto, and Enrique, the details were subsequently overheard the next day by one of the nuns during the freshman class of The Middle Way.

The resultant punishment doled out by the Abbess entailed a three-day retreat during which the girls were woken up at four a.m. to perform 300 bows, chant, engage in sitting meditation, then execute working meditation in the form of scrubbing every floor in the main hall, Buddha Hall, dorms, dining hall and kitchen by hand on their knees. After this, they would complete 300 more bows and chant and sit before bed at twelve a.m., and then start again four hours later.

The Abbess, in her great compassionate wisdom, was determined to rid the two delinquents of their Earthly attachment to that wolf-pack of pelvic thrusting troubadours.

It was a noble effort, because Dorcas, insane with jealousy after viewing the footage of the concert later, tore apart their dorm room searching for the genetically enhanced flower that was guaranteed to not wilt for up to twenty-five years. Dorcas was convinced that *she* would have received the rose, had she been conscious. On top of which, Dorcas was the fan, not Lex. She had no idea that when Lex had been standing on the stage, imprisoned by Enrique's musical lasso and frozen beneath the force of his magnetic gaze, she had tumbled head over heels in love, although she would not admit that until years later.

Try as she might, Dorcas was never able to find the precious flower that Lex felt had been divinely meted out to her alone, since providence had seen fit to pluck Dorcas cleanly from the equation. The Forever-Rose feud nearly ended their friendship, but eventually they got tired of being mad at each other, which was a good thing, because though that particular Pinoy love did, indeed, live on, it was, ultimately, much more ephemeral than the girls' profound respect and affection for one another.

As the crowd below the aerolite swelled past ten times the arena's numbers, Lex smiled to herself and kneaded her knapsack, feeling the rose's shape inside. She didn't know why she had brought it with her on this journey. She just knew that it, along with her mother's brush, alleviated a lingering sense of loneliness. She whispered, "Oh, how sterling," and continued to gaze out, entranced.

Winchester's aerolite flew on for a while then executed a long arc, gradually removing Times Square from Lex's line of sight. She turned from the window and sat back with a sigh. Soon after, the vehicle peeled from the flow and swooped toward the massive Sutton Towers. It circled then gently landed on a platform about halfway up the mile-high building. The door swung open and Lex sprang out.

As Harry turned to follow, Winchester grabbed his arm.

"Hey, Harry. We're settled, you and me. I don't owe you nothin'. We ain't partners and we ain't friends." Winchester stared unblinkingly, bringing his point home, as Harry gazed silently back. He released Harry's arm with a huff, closed the door, and lifted off. Harry followed the aerolite's progress, lost in thought. Then he turned and walked down the landing platform, joining Lex at the front door.

CHAPTER 17

Lex glanced at Harry, trying to hide her anxiety. "No answer."

"Link, access."

"Done."

"Who's Link?"

The front door clicked open and creaked backward into darkness. Maneuvering Lex behind him, Harry raised his rifle and cautiously stepped forward.

"Link, power?"

The lights flickered on a beautifully appointed great room featuring a white baby grand piano, plush furnishings, and a gas fireplace that ignited a fake log. An elegant, curving staircase spiraled to a second floor.

"Dad!" Lex pushed past Harry who lunged for her. "Wow, this is posh!"

Harry whispered tersely, "Wait!" as she rushed toward the piano. She paused with her hand resting on the closed lid while Harry swept the room. "Look at this." She walked around the instrument, studying it from all angles. "I wonder if Dad requested it." She made a face. "Mom had a black one. White's so flashy."

Suddenly, she bolted for the stairs as Harry whispered, "Wait!" again, a little louder. Lex stopped on the stairway, one hand on the polished wooden railing. "There's nobody here," she said with certainty. She turned and bounded away. Harry followed.

On the second floor, Harry strode down a short hall past the master bedroom, stopped, and backed up. Lex sat on the edge of a bed holding a double picture frame. She rubbed her arm over her face roughly, smearing away tears. She sniffled and flashed a class photo of herself and one of a raven-haired woman at Harry.

"That's my mother."

Harry stood in the doorway, ill at ease.

"Her name was Eleanor. My dad called her one of the all-time classic beauties. *Classic.*" She laughed, sniffling. "She died when I was born."

"Negative, Harry. I've accessed the cloud. Date of death was five years before the brat was born."

"Scan the apartment mainframe. Check the dumped files for anything. Maybe a message."

Lex lingered on the picture.

"Dorcas was always jealous, even though she never met her. She thought my mom was beautiful." Lex kept talking to the photo without looking at Harry. "Her mom has this huge mole right under her nose and one of her eyes is walleyed. Dorcas is really mean about all that when she's mad at her mom." Lex looked up. "I don't care who you're talking to anymore," she told Harry. "My dad's the only family I've got, so we're gonna find him."

"Somebody remote flushed most of the data, but there's an encrypted morsel."

"What is it?"

"Axiom BioMolecular, a subsidiary of Fiske Industries."

Harry appeared thoughtful. "That fits." He turned and walked back down the hallway.

"Right. I'll get a location."

Lex closed the picture frame and shoved it into her bag. She wiped her face once more and stood. "Let's find the kitchen," she enthused with the flexibility of youth, all sentimentality gone for the moment. "I gotta eat something." She and Harry trotted down the stairs with Lex right behind him. He stopped abruptly, and Lex bounced off his back.

"Kitchen's that way, kumquat," a familiar voice called from below.

Lex peeked out from behind Harry.

Marlowe lounged in a chair near the fireplace, swirling a drink, flanked by Barry and Vido, who did not look happy. Barry's head and hands were wrapped in bandages while Vido's right arm sported a sling.

Harry cocked his head, listening to Link.

"My bad, Harry. I was accessing the cloud. They must've come in through the servants' entrance."

"You wanna . . . " Marlowe gestured gallantly with his drink, "come join me?"

Lex stayed behind Harry, glued to his back. He began to descend again, one step at a time, and she followed in slow motion. Barry scowled and Vido reached under his jacket with his good arm, but Marlowe waved them down.

"No, no, guys. Come on. I'm certain we can come to an understanding peacefully, hmm, mechanical man?"

"He's not a Mech. He's an android!" shouted Lex from the stairs.

"Feisty ain't she? Listen up, Mech, you took out Parish, so I feel I owe you. Hand over the girl, and I'll forget we ever met. Whaddaya say? Deal?"

When they reached the bottom floor, Harry began to back toward the front door with Lex in tow. Marlowe swirled his drink, sniffed the glass, and helped himself to a leisurely sip.

"Nowhere to go but down, and it's a long way down. Besides, all she wants is to see her daddy. All I want is what she wants." He shrugged magnanimously, drawing in Vido and Barry. "I'm *easy*. EASY. Ain't I, boys?"

"You're the best, Boss," Vido confirmed affectionately.

"No one better," Barry said, glaring murderously across the room. The fire in the fireplace extinguished silently then a faint whistle of escaping gas skated on a lower register just below their voices. Still, Barry ceased glaring and cocked his head. He opened his mouth . . .

"*Harry, get ready to run.*"

A loud scoff like hocking mucus assaulted the hoodlums' ears. Distracted, Barry stopped listening to the strange sound and snapped his head toward the girl, resuming his death glare. Lex leaned out from behind Harry. "Yeah, right, so you threw me in front of a train?!" She mimicked Marlowe's exaggerated shrug.

In a flash, Marlowe was on his feet, his glass shattering on the fake log. Lex cowered, gripping the back of Harry's duster.

"You screwed up my hair! Nobody touches my hair!" Marlowe's distorted face relaxed slowly, micro muscle by micro muscle. He started to smile. "But maybe we're even." He pushed a hand into his tresses, combed it back twice, then added an unnecessary head flip. "Nice bruise you got there." His smirk widened. "Oops!" His hand flew to his mouth. "Hope it doesn't hurt too much, pumpkin. Next time, SHUT IT."

He belly laughed, slapping himself on the leg, and Vido and Barry joined in, guffawing as if they were attending a comedy club.

Harry slowly, continuously kept backing them up. Lex popped out again. "Where's my father, you freakinoid?"

Vido and Barry's hilarity evaporated. They faced each other at the same time, frowning, and Barry's head was cocked again, listening. Marlowe's eyes darted around, eventually landing on the fireplace.

"What the hell is that?"

"*Jig's up, Harry—now!*"

Harry spun Lex toward the front door as the ignitor sparked. A fireball roared into life, engulfed the goons in a hellish blaze, and blew Marlowe through the staircase balusters. Harry slammed the door shut and faced the empty landing pad. He jogged forward to the edge and looked down, seeing nothing but the street almost a mile beneath them.

"*Harry, seven o'clock!*"

Harry adjusted his visual angle to a crane five stories below at a renovation site. It was just starting to swing in their direction.

"I see it."

Harry tossed Lex over a shoulder and hoisted his rifle.

"Wha-what are you doing!"

Harry jumped off the platform.

"HEEEEEEYYYYYY!"

A shriek pumped from Lex's lungs as they plummeted. Her nails clawed his coat. She lost her voice. The duster cracked in her ears and the wind howled as they dropped. Edifices and lights and dark windows blurred by. Suddenly a thud and a clang, and their fall was arrested. Lex's head snapped down, her chin slamming into Harry's back. Now they were whipping horizontally through the air. After an eternity, or only seconds, Harry was jumping down, pounding onto a roof that had appeared out of nowhere. At least to Lex, who hadn't seen it, and she'd had her eyes closed anyway. Harry set her down.

Wobbling on trembling legs, she turned to see the crane and cable Harry had dropped onto and ridden across the chasm. Her gullet heaved and for the first time today she was glad she hadn't eaten.

Movement caught her eye. Five stories above, both Harry and Lex watched as Marlowe, his hair singed to blood-red stubble, lurched into view at the edge of the platform, his face murderous, while Barry and Vido gasped and coughed, their suits smoldering. Marlowe pointed a stiff finger menacingly at Harry and held it there, even as a rooftop elevator chimed softly behind them and the door opened, gently inviting.

"Your chariot has arrived, my good man."

"C'mon!"

Harry yanked Lex into the box and pressed L. Slowly, the doors closed on the smoking thugs, Marlowe, and Marlowe's rigid, accusatory finger. Down in the lobby, a few people eyed the tall, severe-looking man with the rifle and the harried-looking girl with the bruised cheek askance but minded their own business, engaging in traditional Empire City behavior. Harry and Lex emerged through the building's revolving door and made the street, dodging between cars and rickshaws and racing robotic messengers. Eventually, they reached a ramp zigzagging into the depths of the dry East River and sprinted down into the uneven darkness below.

CHAPTER 18

Lex and Harry wound their way through hills of garbage piled a story high on all sides, stepping carefully over unidentifiable lumps, random puddles of rancid smelling liquid, and sharp wooden and glass shards. Lex pulled her blazer up over her nose while Harry continued forward, head on a swivel, oblivious to the rank odor.

A brazen rat crept to the middle of the path, sat up and began to gnaw on something in its paws. Lex squealed and threw herself against Harry who didn't seem to notice. The rat watched them, chewing placidly, as Lex skittered past, latched to Harry's arm. Once safely past the animal, she let go and hugged herself. Their footsteps thudded in the dirt.

"Is this a garbage dump?"

"Yes."

Lex hefted her knapsack and shrugged it onto her back. Her mind bounced about, unmoored. Even though they were on solid ground, the feeling of plunging down, down, down suddenly consumed her, and she stopped, dizzy and nauseated. Harry paused, watching while she bent over, hands on her knees, taking deep breaths. Once she straightened, he immediately started to walk again. Sighing, she had to jog to catch up. She waited for the falling sensation to return, but it seemed to have ebbed … for now. They walked for a long time, heading deeper and deeper into the dump until Lex couldn't take it anymore.

"Hey." Why was she the only one who seemed to hate uncomfortable silences? "Why aren't you called like Robo-tor or Mechanico or something?" She kicked a rock. She would make him talk, whether he wanted to or not. "What kinda name's Harry for a robot—sorry, I mean android?"

A pause ensued as Harry gathered patience.

Oh, questions annoy him, not arm grabbing, she thought, and rolled her eyes.

"I activated about a kilometer that way," he eventually responded, jerking a thumb behind him.

Lex spun around to look and saw nothing. She spun back.

"In a junk pile?"

Harry stared forward as he walked. "I made my way to city services and the caseworker called me another Hard Luck Harry with a sob story."

"You named yourself."

"I had no designation, and my memory was wiped."

Lex absorbed this. Then, "That's so sad."

"Cue the violin music," suggested Link.

Little by little, shacks and lean-tos made of the dregs and dross of society began to appear, at first peppering the austere landscape then crowding together the further they went: rotten wood beams lashed together with wire and computer cables, faded, torn tents flapping in the slight breeze, corrugated iron roofs laid haphazardly over stacks of crates.

Oil drum fires threw jumping shadows along the worn-down dirt paths, outlining the destitute occupants as they watched the strangers vacantly. The abject poverty continued to emerge, its boundaries expanding, no end in sight. As the miserable conditions were revealed, Lex's falling PTSD vanished entirely, displaced by disbelief and sorrow.

"What is this place, Harry?"

"Undertown," Harry stated flatly. "Where humans are dumped."

Lex threw a scant glance his way. "How can people live like this?"

"They scavenge the waste of others. That's how they survive."

Impatiently scrubbing tears away again, Lex scowled at Harry.

"Don't you feel any compassion?"

"Let's cry a river for the vagrants," Link murmured.

Harry's remote expression underscored his answer.

"I don't feel . . . anything."

Lex trudged in his wake, her soul heavy. Something Chihuahua-sized skittered in her peripheral vision but when she looked, it was gone. They passed an elderly man who resembled Lex's father lying beneath a plastic tarp, a dog curled up at his side. She squinted down at him, eyes brimming. It wasn't her father. But he might be somebody's father. Somebody's husband or brother. He was somebody's son.

"Where are we going anyway?" she asked with renewed anxiety.

"Jasper's."

"That guy you paid?"

"My mechanic." Harry kicked an object out of the way. "I found a location where I calculate a strong probability we'll find your father. Axiom Biomolecular, near The Cloisters. We need a vehicle." Harry continued walking and speaking to the air in front of him. "There's probably an APB out on us. Our identification has likely been transmitted to every cab and public conveyance by now."

Lex stopped abruptly and looked at Harry as if seeing him for the first time.

"You calculate . . . "

She stared, her thoughts spinning. Then seeing something beyond him, she suddenly rushed toward what would be the center of town and stopped before the statue of a goddess holding a symbolic jug of nectar, encircled with offerings of rotting fruit, withered flowers, and a few flickering candles.

Lex kneeled and prayed silently as Harry joined her.

He watched for several seconds then asked, "What are you doing?"

"What does it look like?" She glanced up, annoyed. "I'm praying to the Bodhisattva."

"Does it serve a purpose?"

Lex huffed and sat back on her heels.

"A Bodhisattva vows to take on the suffering of others and suffer instead. I'm asking her to help these people."

The wind rustled the plastic tarps and trash around them lightly. "Suffering?"

Huffing again, Lex bent her neck to look up at him. Somewhere in the darkness, voices murmured softly.

"The nuns at school say that all desire leads to suffering. When you let go of your ego's desires, you stop suffering."

Harry processed that. Then, "I'm not human. I don't have an ego." He blinked. "What's its function?"

Lex faced the Bodhisattva again, lips moving rapidly, then pressed her palms together and bowed her head.

"Everybody's got a voice in their head that's always got some opinion about people and stuff that makes you do things or want things you don't need." She stood up, dusting herself off. "Its function is to get you in trouble, most of the time."

Harry was jolted. "A voice." His eyes focused inward. "Yes," he said quietly.

"Not this mumbo-jumbo again."

"At least you're half-right," she concluded. "You're not human."

A distant thunderclap rolled through the night and a burst of fireworks popped and echoed, attracting spectators even here in the ruined, discarded edges of what once was. People wandered from the shadows and peered around the rusted edges of their dwellings, watching the spectacle blossom in the night sky over Empire City, ushering in the new year.

Harry and Lex were both drenched in brilliant, shifting colors.

Feeling lost and somewhat hopeless, she faced him despondently as the fireworks crackled and whistled.

"Well, Happy New Year . . . *robot.*"

Harry started to turn her way. Piercing feedback erupted in his ears. He grabbed one side of his head and sank to his knees, eyes screwed shut. Mortified, Lex dropped beside him.

"I didn't mean to call you a robot! I was just mad! I'm sorry!"

Slicing cleanly through the feedback, a voice invaded his head. *"Mechanoid, I'm transmitting on your frequency, so I know you hear me."*

Harry fell to his back and rolled around in excruciating pain, hands mashed against his skull.

"You've stolen what belongs to me, and I want it returned immediately or others will suffer for your belligerence."

Miles above the fireworks and the milling masses of Empire City, Fiske held Harry's life ruthlessly in the palm of his hand. As English assisted him in the control room, he offered a few paltry seconds of warning: "Here is a taste, my mechanized friend."

A computer-generated map located Harry in Undertown, blinking and chiming. Without hesitation, Fiske yanked a handle and pressed a button.

***

Clouds boiled with hot power as a bolt of energy blew a crater in the dirt just outside Undertown and slashed a huge furrow toward the shantytown. Back at Times Square, as confetti rained in torrents, the revelers gasped and cheered in delight at the unexpected light show taking place a mile away. It was like a bolt of lightning straight from heaven, portending an auspicious start to the new year.

***

In Undertown, the homeless stampeded blindly, gripped by panic. Lex helped Harry to his feet as the statue toppled over and shattered.

"Link, track to source!"

"I'm on it."

As the ground rumbled and quaked, Harry grabbed Lex roughly by the shoulders.

"Run."

Fear rooted her in place.

"RUN!"

Harry shoved her into the stampeding horde and watched her progress before pulling his visor down. He sprinted back toward the garbage dump they'd passed.

"Triangulating . . . "

***

The L-Sat Seven Fiske Industries satellite drifted over Empire City, energy spewing from a barrel.

"It's a satellite! Accessing . . . "

The laser sputtered and died.

"Harry, I can't maintain a lock."

"Realign!"

Fiske's voice boomed in Harry's ears. *"Behold what your meddling has wrought!"*

***

Harry scaled a mountain of trash to its apex, his face twisting in agony.

"The universe is driven by primal forces." Fiske continued pontificating from the safety of the sky. *"Now you must pay for interfering with the one named . . . Solomon Fiske!"*

"Uploading new coordinates!" came Link a second after.

Lex scrambled with the stampede, slipping in the dirt. Pebbles raked across her palms and a foot grazed her ribs, but she felt none of it as she turned to see a cone of light descend from the sky and envelop a tiny figure atop a mountain of garbage.

Breathlessly: "Harry . . . "

Harry stood on the heap surrounded by light.

"Harry? I gotta take you out."

"Why?"

"Orders."

A flash, a rain of debris, a gale force wind, and the entire trash heap disintegrated, replaced by a smoldering crater. Tossed by the concussive shockwave, Lex flew backwards onto her butt. Slowly lifting her eyes, she stared at the aftermath, dazed and mute. A pair of hands yanked her roughly to her feet, bringing her face-to-face with Marlowe, his stubbled, singed head gleaming in the fireworks.

"Hello, sugar dumplin'" he growled.

Lex struggled against Barry who held her in an uncompromising grip. Vido supervised, a gun in his uninjured hand pointed at Lex's stomach. Marlowe sneered at the crater, grinning from ear to ear. "Adios, Mechanical Man!" He saluted the empty air jauntily and strolled away with a pep in his step.

CHAPTER 19

In Fiske's floating estate in the sky, klaxons shrilled and split the night as a heavy-duty aerolite hauled the *Sao Paulo's* armored cargo container into the hangar to be offloaded and secured by a swarm of earmuffed technicians.

Fiske sat in his meeting hall behind the huge marble table slurping at a bootlegged bowl of shark fin soup while an episode of *Nǐ Jīng Cháng Lái Zhè Ma (Do You Come Here Often?)* played, muted, on the gigantic wall screen. FirstTradeView ticker tape ran along the bottom of the screen, as always, where Fiske religiously tracked trending stock market information.

Across from him, a young maid named Dot raised a spoonful of the same soup with a trembling hand, spilling most of it back into the bowl.

Just two weeks ago, the Head Chef had been unable to procure several of the usual shipments of Fiske's favorite illicit foods and had tried a desperate hail Mary—slipping konjac gel, a shark fin imitation, into the dinner menu.

Twelve hours later, when the Head Chef disappeared and a large amount of mystery meat not present on the shipment log had appeared out of nowhere, Dot, along with most of the staff, had abruptly gone vegan. Or at least until the mystery meat had been consumed, mostly by the beefy bodyguards who were too jacked up to care and some of the aerolite chauffeurs who tended to be young and naïve. Even when she'd tried to tell them, face to face, what had most likely become of Madame Robuchon and what their burger was made out of, they'd looked at her testily and told her to take a hike.

As Dot's hand quaked and the spoon clattered against her bowl, Fiske's red, watery eyes dropped from the screen to the maid's ashen face.

Though he enjoyed eating alone most of the time, now and then Fiske wanted company—silent company—and today Dot had drawn the short straw. In the wake of Chef Ghislaine Robuchon's troubling disappearance Dot not only lacked an appetite but was terrified that her rioting stomach would paint the marble table with her earlier lunch.

"Do try to keep the noise down, dear," Fiske said quietly in her direction as his rheumy eyes sought the show again. "I have a headache which persists . . . "

Fiske thought perhaps it had been the excitement of finally ridding himself of that aggravating Mech. His blood pressure couldn't tell the difference between delight and distress, evidently. As something unfolded onscreen, Fiske unloosed a low chuckle.

Dot nodded tersely in acknowledgement, even though he was no longer looking at her. Sweating profusely, she set her spoon down before she dropped it and decided at that moment that this job was not worth it. She would pack her case and ask Rougui in Shipping to sneak her out of here tomorrow—maybe tonight.

Tonight would be good, since it was the New Year. She could see from the old grandfather clock in the corner that it was almost one a.m., and the celebrations and general chaos would provide cover. She chastised herself for not leaving the moment she'd caught sight of the probable Robuchon burgers and steaks two weeks ago.

As Dot swooned in her chair, wondering how she was going to get through the next two courses, Mister English entered the room, stopping just inside the threshold. Fiske looked up, smacking his lips.

"Ah, Mister English." He smeared a champagne-colored linen napkin over his mouth and began to push his chair back. English moved forward quickly to assist him. "It's that time already?" Fiske gazed at the half-full bowl with longing. "I'll finish my meal later, I suppose. Let's get this meet and greet over with."

They started to leave then Fiske, remembering Dot, turned back. "You may return to your duties, my dear. My sincerest gratitude for your company."

The men exited. Dot made herself count to twenty before she sprang to her feet and sprinted from the room, colliding head-on with Chef Robuchon in the foyer. Dot blinked rapidly as Chef righted a wash cart and straightened a starched white laundry uniform with one hand. Relief and confusion warring within her, Dot stood paralyzed until Chef whispered waspishly, "Yes! I got demoted. Life goes on!"

Chef shoved the cart ahead of her as she stomped toward the cleaning facility.

It was a bona fide, twenty-four-carat New Year miracle, but it didn't matter. The emotional and psychological damage had been done. The palpable terror of untold power and its boundless potential for evil had invaded her, belatedly, and she did not appreciate the experience. At all. Dot raced for her room and her suitcase. She never looked back.

***

Fiske and English stood before the hatch as it swung open with a whoosh of air followed by a ramp extending downward. A geriatric husk of a man bound to an electric wheelchair emerged gradually through the condensing mist.

"Senator Moss. It is an honor." Fiske held out his hand and Moss rolled past it.

"Let's do away with formalities, shall we, Fiske? I'm here for my new body."

Apart from a small tic in Fiske's jaw, his expression remained congenial. English moved behind the senator to push the wheelchair and Moss batted him away.

"It's self-propelling. You are redundant," he snapped.

"We're just starting the process," Fiske informed Moss lightly.

"Why hasn't it been grown by now? You're not trying to squeeze more out of the deal, are you?"

Fiske tutted. "Nonsense. I've had unavoidable delays. But nothing to be concerned about."

Moss took several raspy breaths then burst into a painful-sounding hack.

"My lungs . . . aren't used to such an . . . oxygen-rich environment."

"Needless to say," Fiske reminded him, "your new lungs will have no problems in that regard, Senator."

The whooping coughs finally died away.

"Hmm. We'll see."

Moss's expression was sour, doing nothing for his overall appearance which appeared to be five steps from the grave. Fiske observed him in silent distaste, flashes of brown-lipped abalone and Malva pudding parading before his eyes, as he smiled affably, the master of dissimulation.

CHAPTER 20

Jasper was milling steel in the workshop and didn't hear the persistent beeping until he turned the fly cutter off. He was about to yell for Cecil but remembered he'd sent him to Hoboken to retrieve Harry's part.

Straightening and rubbing his back, he realized the sound was coming from the terminal he'd had Harry plugged into earlier. He rushed to the back of the shop and snapped the monitor on. A readout filled the screen: SAFE MODE: CRITICAL SYSTEM FAILURE.

Jasper's eyes widened.

Hustling to the operating room, he emerged seconds later with a satchel. Donning a down jacket over his Cyberwerkz overalls and an old bucket hat, he slipped out the front door and loped unevenly to his van, favoring his good hip. Stressful times like these came very close to seducing him into the world of the cybernetic body parts that he bestowed on everyone else. He could hardly remember what it was like to get up from the floor without wincing or hop off a stool onto flexible knees instead of rigid bundles of frozen ligaments.

Outside, he battled his way through streets flooded with vehicles flying New Years banners and balloons, horns honking, and hundreds of pedestrians packed together, inching forward like a giant organism with no particular destination. Finally, he squeezed his way into some back streets away from the crowds and floored it toward the tracker coordinates.

At the entrance to Undertown, Jasper stopped the van, not trusting the rickety-looking ramp to support a vehicle. He trampled down the zig-zagging slope clinging to his satchel and following a beeping range finder. Shadows emerged from behind piles of trash and flapping tents and watched him run past. Some followed. By the time Jasper began clawing his way up a particular hill of trash, a small audience of Undertown residents circled the bottom, waiting to see what happened.

Jasper reached the crest and gasped at what he saw. The range finder spiraled into rapid beeping.

"Merciful Tathagata!"

He scooted and slid down the side of a huge crater through dirt and cans and boxes and plastic.

"Harry . . . " he murmured, worried, eyes darting. There was nothing in front of him but more and more trash on top of disturbed earth.

Flinging his equipment aside, Jasper dropped to his knees and pawed through the refuse, finding nothing. Desperation set in. From the corner of his eye, he glimpsed a crooked stick, did a double-take. It was a finger. Jasper threw himself over, dug out a hand, then spent the next hectic minutes frantically uncovering Harry's head and back.

Jasper tore off Harry's charred duster and shredded body armor with hands covered in grime and filth, straining to get him on his back. With a final grunt, he shoved Harry over and gazed down into his sightless eyes.

"What in heaven's . . . "

Removing a device from his satchel, he attached a lead to Harry's ear and another to his finger and activated it. A whine like a charging flash filled the air and a spark jumped between Harry's ear and finger. His body bucked.

"Come on, buddy . . . "

Jasper adjusted the voltage and received the same result.

"This'll probably burn out your brain," he muttered, "but . . . "

He amped up the voltage and pressed the button, whispering a quick prayer under his breath.

Harry thrashed violently amidst the dirt and trash then unexpectedly sat up like a marionette. His eyelids stuttered and his head twitched from side to side as he rebooted. Sitting back on his heels, Jasper exhaled long and hard. He watched Harry's juddering head.

"Harry, can you hear me?"

Harry turned in staccato increments.

"J-Jasper . . . " he said in a filtered synthetic voice.

"Yeah, it's me. I'm gonna adjust your power output."

Jasper monkeyed with the microcontrollers and modified the switching regulator, smoothing out Harry's movements as much as possible.

"Can you stand?"

Harry blinked once then began to battle his way to his feet. Spotting his Enforcer, he bent over stiffly, grasped it one-handed and clung loosely to the handle. Jasper grabbed his equipment, threw an arm around Harry's waist, and they both struggled up the crater and down the other side. The ring of waiting Undertown residents parted at the bottom, watching silently as the odd pair staggered up the path that led back to the world.

＊＊＊

The van was still parked on the blighted street above Undertown, and Jasper muttered whispered prayers of thanks. Harry tossed his rifle into the back and climbed unsteadily inside with Jasper following. Jasper guided him to lie prone on a workbench, connected him to a monitor, and went to work on the link. Several tense moments passed in silence as he probed through the mess he was seeing.

"What hit you?"

Harry's body shuddered violently.

"L-L-Lex?"

"Lex? What's that?"

Harry sat up and pulled the leads off the back of his head.

"L-Link? Link, r-respond."

Jasper shook his head. "The link's fried, Harry. We gotta get you back to the shop."

"Funk . . . shun . . . ul." Link's faltering voice filled Harry's ear.

Harry responded, "Locate . . . t-tracking . . . signal."

"Wer . . . king." Pause. *"Sig . . . nal . . . lo . . . kay . . . ted."*

Harry pulled on the visor. It displayed a map of the city where a dot blinked north toward the Cloisters.

"H-have . . . to get . . . L-Lex," Harry stammered.

"You're in no condition to get a pizza, let alone this Lex, whatever that is."

"M-my . . . c-client." Suddenly Harry grabbed Jasper and pulled him close. "P-patch . . . me up."

Jasper studied Harry, alert to his pain. And something else. An intensity bordering on desperation. He sighed, nodding slowly. "Okay, Harry. I'll do what I can."

CHAPTER 21

As Cecil guided the scooter through a parking lot at the Hoboken docks, a limousine parked at the far end flashed its lights. Cecil pulled up beside the blackened rear passenger window and lifted his helmet visor. The window lowered silently.

A shadowy man in the backseat extended a beringed hand and pointed at Cecil.

"You Jasper's boy?"

Cecil frowned but restrained himself from a sarcastic reply. He nodded.

The mysterious occupant extended a cigar box out of the window. Cecil picked it up and flipped the top open, examining the contents. A duplicate of Harry's link lay inside, swaddled in a bundle of crepe wadding.

"Hey, kid. The guy that sold me that asked me to pass along a message."

"Yeah? What's that, pal?"

Satisfied, Cecil closed the box and slipped it into the messenger bag slung across his chest.

"He said, quote, 'Destroy the thing you're trying to repair. Destroy it or live to regret it.' End quote."

Cecil gripped the scooter's handlebars tightly.

"Buddy, my friend needs this, so you better not be sellin' us a piece of crap, or you'll regret meeting *me*."

The driver's door flew open and a giant heaved his alarming bulk to his feet. Very quickly. Cecil started.

"Leave him!" the passenger snapped.

The driver provided Cecil with a menacing head-to-toe once-over then deliberately folded his mass back into the car.

"You ain't too bright," said the shadowy man, "but you got heart. I'll give you that." He snapped his fingers and the limo lifted straight up into the sky. "Happy New Year, kid."

Cecil wrenched the scooter around in a half-circle. "I'm coming, Harry." He took off in the opposite direction, tires screeching.

CHAPTER 22

"Creation is great, and cannot be understood."
–Thomas Carlyle

The Axiom Biomolecular cloning chamber was an incredible achievement, the possibilities fantastic . . . for some. A different perspective might include a more pessimistic view—a nightmarish landscape of processed, warehoused flesh meant only for those diametrically opposite to the discarded, nameless bodies inhabiting Undertown.

Standing on a catwalk above an industrial space expansive enough to house fleets of aerolites, English inspected the giant stainless steel vats and man-sized transparent tanks encased in scaffolding that filled the room. A rhythmic, muted thudding drew his attention to one of the tanks where Lex was hermetically sealed inside. She slammed her palms against the glass periodically shouting, "Let me out!"

Vido stood outside the tank, arm in a new sling, smiling, and tapped the glass with his good finger. Glaring, Lex threw herself against the tube. Vido's smile dimmed a few watts.

"Be careful. That one's a barracuda."

Marlowe sauntered into the warehouse sporting a maroon shoulder-length wig that failed spectacularly to even approach the splendor of his original hair. Barry followed, manhandling someone wearing a lab coat over civilian clothes, a swollen lip marring his face. Lex's mouth dropped open.

"Dad!"

Rosewood lurched toward her and Barry twisted his arm more tightly behind him.

"Alexia," he said softly. Then louder, anguished, "What are you *doing* here?" Then, angrily, seeing her bruise, "How did you receive that injury!"

Inspired by the show of emotion, Barry mashed Rosewood's face into the glass tank.

"If you hurt him . . . " came Lex's muffled yell from behind the glass.

Marlowe glanced at Barry and flicked his wrist. "Hurt him."

Barry redoubled his efforts to fuse Rosewood's skin cells with the tank while yanking his arm higher behind him, nearly breaking it. The doctor moaned, his voice breaking.

"You were sayin', Peanut?" Marlowe tilted his head, lips quirking, as Lex put her hand on the glass over her father's face. "And, oh," he said, turning to Rosewood amicably, "it was me that did that." He pointed at Lex's cheek. "It's your fault. You're a bad father. Teach your brat manners, egghead!"

Rosewood struggled fiercely but Barry yanked his arm up, pinning him in place.

"Enough, enough!" Fiske's voice boomed into the room. Barry immediately loosened his hold on the doctor's arm. Everyone turned to see Fiske's corpulent face appear on the large screen above the chamber. Marlowe positioned himself beside a red valve next to Lex's tank as Fiske continued speaking.

"It's time you finish the task you've been so handsomely compensated for, Dr. Rosewood. Wouldn't you say, sir?"

Barry scoffed and nodded in agreement.

The doctor didn't respond.

In the background, Fiske nodded at Marlowe who eagerly turned the valve.

"Hey," Marlowe said gently, leaning forward toward Lex. "Thirsty?"

In the bottom of the tank water surged from an opening, quickly sloshing over Lex's shoes.

Rosewood raised his voice, appealing to the Boss of Empire City. "Please . . . "

Barry tightened his grip cruelly, but subtly, so Fiske wouldn't see.

"I'll do what you want." Rosewood gasped, barely able to speak through compressed ribs.

"Oh, I'm aware of that, Doctor. You *will* do what I want. But I'm glad it's all out in the open now." He delivered a beneficent smile to the room in general.

"Take her out of there," Rosewood wheezed. "Please!"

Fiske made a grand show of turning over his wrist as if an old-fashioned watch was there. He pantomimed reading the invisible watch and then said, "I'd say she has twenty minutes before she drowns, Doctor. Get to work!"

Barry released Rosewood and shoved him to the floor.

Massaging his aching arm, Rosewood stood up slowly. He and Lex locked eyes for a few terrible seconds then he tore himself away. At a table a few feet from her tank, he selected several labeled canisters, opened them, and began to combine them in a vial. His eyes darted distractedly toward the tube as the water reached Lex's ankles. Above Rosewood another video screen blinked on beside Fiske, displaying Moss's sour, anemic countenance.

"Senator," Fiske announced, "I thought you'd like to witness the process."

"Is that her?" Moss squinted down at the scene below.

"Yes, Senator, that is her. The first fully viable human clone in history." Fiske's voice blasted loudly over the speakers, echoing throughout the warehouse. "Although the donor, in this case the doctor's late wife," he continued, conversationally, "expired as a consequence of Amyotrophic Lateral Sclerosis, her clone shows no sign of the disease. Neither does she suffer shortened telomeres."

Lex straightened rigidly in the tube as the water surrounded her shins.

"We've spoken briefly about telomeres, Senator. The DNA protein structures on the ends of chromosomes that protect from nucleolytic degradation?" Moss made no response and Fiske cleared his throat. "Well, her DNA is aging normally," he stated with assurance. "In your case, the doctor has repaired the damage to the sample you provided. You have no idea of the ordeal and considerable cost smuggling it accrued—"

Moss exploded.

"Don't haggle with me, Fiske! You're about to gain an entire planet to exploit. Now get on with it."

"Of course, Senator," Fiske rejoined soothingly. "There will be no trace of your radiation poisoning. None whatsoever in your new body."

Moss fixed on Lex unblinkingly, his expression inhuman and ravenous.

"Wondrous," he whispered, but everyone heard him clearly.

In the tank, Lex watched her father with growing incredulity. He continued to work, not looking at her.

"What the hell are they talking about?" Lex's muffled voice rose. "I'm not a clone, Dad. Tell them!"

Agitated, Rosewood carefully filled a large syringe with the final combination of elements. He shot her a quick look. "It's all right, Alexia. I can explain—"

"Oh . . . !" Fiske chortled onscreen, his cheeks rising to blot out his eyes. "Seems I've let the *clone* out of the bag, so to speak. I assumed she knew what she was. Ha." He shook his head in amusement. "How rich. How rich, indeed."

Lex stood unmoving, face blank, then slowly dropped into the water until she was sitting down. She knew this couldn't be a prank or some sick joke. Her father had been born without a sense of humor. If you told him a joke or some witty pun, he would just stand there blinking. Rosewood was a man of formulas and equations, not a comedian. Which led Lex to a gut-wrenching conclusion . . .

Lex, still sitting on the bottom of the tank with the water lapping at her chest, whispered to herself, "I'm not a real person either. I'm sorry, Harry."

She watched as her father approached an adjacent tank and climbed the ladder to its hatch. He stabbed the syringe into an injection port, emptying it into a translucent bladder hanging inside, then returned to the floor where he engaged in a dizzying range of data entry tasks, manipulating a sea of knobs and levers and buttons.

"You expect me to wait nine months for it to mature?" Moss's voice was feeble but housed a dangerous undertone.

"Oh, no, no, Senator, no, no," Fiske responded, unaffected. "Such are the miracles of modern science. Fiske Industries' chemical division has developed Mutagen X, a growth accelerant."

Moss's beady eyes bounced through the warehouse until they landed on a large open vat labeled Mutagen X in bright neon green.

"A proprietary formula. It will do wonders on Mars with livestock and fish. Food shortages will be a thing of the past." Fiske was pleased with his philanthropic aspirations. He could see the veneration and respect shining up at him from here. *But the body business will be the real miracle,* he thought, *because nobody wants to die.*

Rosewood stood at a console monitoring readouts and making micro-adjustments as a bizarre metamorphosis began. Everyone present watched through the glass as a microscopic egg in the bladder became visible, growing into a zygote then an embryo, quickly transforming into a fetus. In moments it was the size of a newborn baby, maturing impossibly fast.

Onscreen, Moss's desiccated face radiated wonder.

"I see . . . " he murmured.

CHAPTER 23

The guardhouse was situated at the edge of an industrial park.

The security guard yawned and stretched expansively while watching a small TV with the volume down low. His back popped and he grimaced, reaching around to rub it. He bent from side to side then did a few shallow twists. He snickered at something onscreen as headlights swept across his face. His head popped up. He grabbed a machine gun and stepped out, raising a hand as Jasper's van rolled to a stop.

"Evening, Officer," Jasper said nervously, trying to sound casual.

The guard bent down and aimed a flashlight first at Jasper then across the seat at Harry who sat trembling, dressed in a baseball cap and undersized Cyberwerkz overalls that strained across his chest and thighs.

"No trespassing."

"Got a call 'bout a broken three el seven dynabot." Jasper paused to clear his throat. "Burned out a servo." He was doing a horrible acting job and the guard sensed it. On top of that, Harry shaking like a palsy victim was not helping.

"I gotta call it in," the guard told them. He removed a radio from a holster around his waist. "This is the front gate. I got a couple of repair guys out here to fix some Mech. Copy?"

As the guard waited for a response, Harry exited the van and headed toward him unsteadily, the too-short pant legs flapping above his ankles.

Alarmed, the guard barked, "Get back inside the—" and Harry coldcocked him. Jasper flinched and eyed the fallen man grimly.

"Is that what you do for a living? Beat people up?"

"Help me."

Jasper climbed out reluctantly and helped Harry drag the man's dead weight to the back of the van.

The radio snapped on. *"Front gate, front gate. We have nothing scheduled."*

Harry picked the radio up with trembling fingers and spoke in the security guard's voice.

"Wrong address."

"Right."

Jasper stared. "How'd you do that? I didn't know you could do that."

Harry bent over and began yanking the guard's uniform off.

"Jasper, change."

Jasper balked, on the verge of panic. "I don't think I'd be very believable—"

"Jasper!"

Jasper exhaled all of the air from his lungs and began to change unenthusiastically. Harry secured the guard with patch cord then tossed him into the back of the van. He handed Jasper the guard's hat and radio, all business.

"Wait here," he instructed.

"What do I do if somebody shows up?" He glanced around in all the directions anyone could appear from.

Harry held the machine gun out. "Point and shoot."

Jasper accepted the gun, holding it awkwardly. After a long pause he said, "I don't need this karma," but he said it to the air, because Harry was already driving away.

***

Jasper's van pulled up in front of Axiom Biomolecular's main entrance where a second security guard occupied a receptionist's desk. He was watching TV also, a small device hidden out of sight, and was annoyed to be pulled away from the game. He could hear the crowds cheering as he headed for the front doors and snapped on his radio.

"Front gate? I thought you said it was a wrong address."

There was a long silence.

"*Uh . . .* " Jasper coughed and cleared his throat tensely, *"that's a twenty-four seven."*

The guard approached the driver's side and found it empty. He leaned forward cautiously to open the door, and a hand reached down from the van's roof and ripped him off his feet.

***

In the cloning chamber, no longer able to sit, Lex stood, teeth chattering, as the water swirled around her waist. Rosewood monitored and adjusted readings and controls frantically, keeping one eye on the water flooding Lex's tank. The clone continued to grow steadily, looking around the age of sixteen.

"Fiske, the clone is almost grown. Drain that water from the tank—please!"

Fiske was unconcerned. "She looks like a strong swimmer," came his airy reply. Taking the statement to heart, Marlowe twisted the wheel further and water rushed into Lex's tank faster. A computer terminal began to beep and flash insistently, drawing Rosewood to the readout. He whirled around.

"It's done, Fiske!"

"Mister English," Fiske said on-screen.

English pulled a lever on a console. A loud clunk reverberated, rattling glass vials, then the roof began to retract.

Outside, an aerolite's engines thrummed as it positioned itself over the opening and lowered a thick cable. Hearing it, Harry looked up as he finished securing the second guard, quickly leapt straight up onto the roof, then hurled himself off onto the cable.

"Mister English, secure the clone," instructed Fiske.

Suddenly, everything happened at once.

"Not possible!" Marlowe wailed, pointing. "It's alive! Destroy it!" he screamed at Barry and Vido. Harry slung himself off the thick wire in a controlled arc to the catwalk as Mister English vaulted onto the cable and slid down to the top of the clone's enclosure. The goons tore their guns free, firing with abandon, as Harry raced around the catwalk toward Lex's tank. A hail of bullets pinged against expensive machinery and industrial drums.

"Harry!" Treading water, Lex struggled to keep her chin above the surface. All Marlowe saw when he looked at the girl was the destroyer of the most cherished and hard-won asset of his life. Spotting an oversized wrench leaning against the railing, he didn't think twice before grabbing it and smashing it down on the water valve. It cracked and the handle snapped off. Marlowe sprinted for the catwalk access ladder, wrench in hand.

Catching Marlowe's maliciousness amidst the chaos, Fiske yelled angrily, "Marlowe! I need the girl alive!"

Harry dove behind a drum and checked his Enforcer as bullets punched the air and drilled the walls.

"The doctor, Mister English!" called Fiske, feeling the first questing tendrils of alarm uncoiling within him. Everything had been going so swimmingly. How had chaos entered so fast and taken control? He had worked too hard for this. Suddenly a warm calm came over him, a sense of prescience flooding his very soul, and he was rock solid again. No one could stop him. No one could stop this. This was greatness beyond anyone's understanding.

Fiske watched English attach the aerolite's cable to the top of the tank. Dropping down to the tank's console, he yanked up hard on a lever, detaching pipes and cables in a spray of sparks and hissing gas vapor, then signaled the vehicle. It thrust upward, lifting the entire platform into the air behind it.

Mister English grabbed Rosewood by the neck.

"Alexia!" Rosewood struggled mightily against the hulking valet to reach Lex. Almost completely underwater, she dog paddled in a frenzy, her mouth pressed against the top of the enclosure, sucking in the last of the air.

As the clone's tank rose slowly, Harry fired several smoke grenades from the Enforcer against its bottom. They bounced to the floor, filling the immediate area with thick smoke, momentarily blinding Barry and Vido. Controlling his spasms with a force of will, Harry aimed and fired a grenade that beelined into Barry's groin. He pinwheeled, crashing backwards, knocked out cold.

"Link! Stop that transport!"

"*S-s-system failure. Voice not recognized. Reset parameters. Please repeat.*"

Harry ducked as Marlowe charged, the wrench swinging for his temple.

"Look what you did to me, you mechanized freak!" he screamed. Gunfire erupted, and Marlowe's ill-fitting wig flew off. He rounded on Vido who was firing wildly from the smoke below.

"You blind?! Shoot *him*!"

Marlowe turned back around straight into Harry's fist. Reeling, he bumped into a button, and a shrieking klaxon rent the air. Harry pivoted unsteadily, quickly firing a net at Vido who was swept off his feet and flung across the room at velocity.

In the tank, Lex was now underwater holding her breath, eyes bulging, feebly pounding the glass. Marlowe rushed forward swinging wide with the wrench. Harry ducked and Marlowe flipped over the railing and splashed into the vat of Mutagen X. Springing off the catwalk, Harry landed on the scaffolding of Lex's tank and twisted the hatch wheel, but it wouldn't budge.

Lifting his head, he glimpsed Moss on the video screen, his eyes fixed on Lex. Harry turned back to the hatch wheel and froze. Slowly, he looked back at the screen. His hands dropped from the wheel. The warehouse vanished as a roaring tunnel vision made the world go dark and pinned Moss in the center of an empty, black space. Harry blinked, poised on the edge of a ghostly memory that haunted the dim recesses of his neural pathways, hidden in a shadowy corner, but it skittered away to regions unknown. Unknowable. Sequestered. Forbidden.

Marlowe sluggishly pulled himself out of the vat. He slopped to the floor, coated in viscous, slimy oil, snapping Harry back to his senses. Facing the tank, he gripped the wheel and twisted, throwing his whole body weight into it, teeth bared. Suddenly, with a sharp crack, the wheel snapped off.

Harry dropped to his knees, drained, and looked down, locking eyes with Lex.

Marlowe moaned and leaned forward, hands on his knees, swaying. Suddenly, a giant glob of goo poured from his mouth as his arms, legs and torso swelled, ripping his clothing to shreds in seconds. In a matter of moments, he'd grown big enough for his head to smash through the catwalk, sending it thundering down, along with the two giant video screens.

Up above, English, Rosewood, and the tank cleared the open roof and quickly disappeared into the night sky.

Forcing his fingers into the hatch edges with trembling hands, Harry strained with Herculean effort, as if tearing himself apart. His neck and arms bulged obscenely, accompanied by popping and snapping sounds.

A phalanx of security guards stormed into the warehouse with machine guns drawn as the squeal of breached metal pierced the air. The hatch tore off and Harry hurled it then dropped to his belly and plunged his arms into the water. He grabbed Lex by her blazer and quickly wrenched her out. Water streamed from her mouth as she coughed and gasped, scrabbling blindly to clutch his arms.

The security guards cocked their weapons and Harry paused, taking in the semicircle of armed men. As Lex coughed up more water, Harry pulled her close, rapidly ticking through options. Link was damaged. There would be no help there.

Maybe if he . . .

A rumble quaked the air.

The guards turned as one toward Marlowe's swollen, fifteen-foot body in astonishment. Immediately dropping their weapons, they prostrated themselves along the floor in blind religious awe, as though in the presence of a living god.

"The Buddha!" half of them murmured in unison. The other half were speechless.

Marlowe looked strikingly like the laughing Buddha in Times Square.

His mouth dropped open, expelling a deafening belch. The echo died away, leading into an extended silence. The guards watched in confusion as Marlowe's giant body first tilted then began to plummet toward them. Screams rebounded against the walls.

Lex buried her face in Harry's chest away from the sound of an enormous splash and a wave of gooey liquid that sloshed against the tank. The guards slipped and slid amid a slimy pool of what was once Preston Marlowe.

"I thought you were gone," Lex said, and burst into tears.

Harry cradled her, his whole body quaking, jumped off the tank, and set her down. Casting briefly about for her skull and bones bag, Lex located it on top of a console and snatched it up. Together they rushed out.

CHAPTER 24

Jasper stood inside the guardhouse peering nervously through the glass, his body as taut as a wire. If someone showed up, he had no idea what he was going to do, because there was no way he was going to visit violence upon them.

At first he hummed his way nervously through a slew of calming song titles, but even *Jack Your World* didn't help quell the strain. Then muttering some of Moksha's most famous quotes to himself only started to annoy him, and he suddenly recognized in a lightbulb-going-off moment that she was nothing but a shyster.

"Enlightenment is like a basket of day-old lemons." "Empathy is the soul's negativity purgative." It was like she'd stolen a crate of fortune cookies and plagiarized a thousand dessert aphorisms, changing them slightly to shoe-horn them into her ambiguous esoteric brand. She'd been around for so long and was so familiar her phrases had become part of the lexicon.

But she wasn't real. At least to him. As of this moment. Millions of others adored her, though, and he had been one of those just two seconds ago. *Was she real or not real?* Jasper wondered, warming to the mental argument he was having with himself. Maybe it didn't matter what he thought. Maybe it was just a matter of perception. Maybe "real" was only a construct but could also evolve beyond its beginnings. He felt better thinking about these things instead of pacing and worrying in a stranger's clothes, his stomach clenched like a rock.

In the distance a pair of headlights appeared out of the darkness, bouncing toward him from Axiom Biomolecular. All thoughts of Moksha and fortune cookies and the evolution of being evaporated as Jasper watched the vehicle approach, tensing for confrontation and not prepared for violence. When he realized it was his van, hot relief rushed through him.

He ran out, still holding the machine gun, as the van came to a dusty stop outside the guardhouse. He did a double take at his hands and dropped the machine gun in disgust. He rounded the back of the vehicle where a young girl watched as Harry shoved the security guards out onto the road with the last of his strength. Shaking his head, Jasper climbed into the driver's seat, waited for the girl to get in, and stomped the accelerator. In the back, Harry collapsed in a convulsing heap.

Lex threw herself down beside him.

"What's wrong with him?"

Jasper said, "He's dying, kid." He didn't look back.

Lex's face crumpled in helpless stages. She grabbed onto one of Harry's flopping hands and held tight. Twenty-four minutes of negligent back street driving later, Jasper sped down the block toward Cyberwerkz. Duesenberg was ringing the door buzzer as the van skidded to a halt. Jasper bolted out of the driver's seat, heading toward the back.

"Doozy, gimme a hand!"

Jasper flung the back doors open, revealing Harry on the floor shaking wildly. Duesenberg froze, not knowing what to do.

"Ganapati!" he cried.

"Help him!" Lex wailed.

Jasper tossed a key-card at Lex and with Duesenberg's help heaved Harry out of the van and to his feet. Despite the hour, the sidewalk was teeming with activity. Passersby steered clear of the commotion, veering away and avoiding eye contact. A little girl stopped to ogle Harry and a boy only slightly older than her yanked her away by the arm.

"Open the door, kid!" Jasper's knee buckled painfully under Harry's weight as Lex swiped the door. He and Duesenberg half-dragged, half-carried Harry inside to the operating table.

"What's happening to him?" Duesenberg was breathing hard. He patted his coat pockets in a frenzy, searching for his chewable antacid pills.

Jasper quickly hooked up leads, wiring the back of Harry's head and forehead. He ripped the Cyberwerkz coveralls open, the Velcro tearing loudly, and attached more leads to his chest.

"His brain is collapsing under the weight of that link."

"Link?" Lex looked at Harry. "The guy he's always talking to?"

"It's not a guy." Jasper finished the wiring. "It's himself."

Duesenberg found the pills and tossed his head back, swallowing them whole. He pulled off his coat and hat and tossed them in a corner. "Tell me what to do, Jasper."

Jasper handed Duesenberg a read-out device.

"I'm gonna try and stabilize his neural processors. Monitor this reading, and if it goes anywhere below twenty-five, yell!"

Duesenberg nodded nervously while Lex pressed her hands together painfully. Jasper accessed the link and got to work. But not before he lifted his head and yelled, "Where the hell is Cecil?!"

***

Under a night sky brilliant with fireworks, Cecil fought the jam-packed traffic, completely stressed out.

"Come on!" His voice was swallowed by the surrounding mayhem like an insect down the maw of an immense creature. "Move-your-freakin'-car!"

Gunning the scooter, he jumped the curb, extended his free arm and his legs, and thrashed them around wildly, snake-like.

"Deranged Mech! I'm CRAZY! Look out!" Cecil yelled at the top of his lungs, deeply satisfied to see alarmed pedestrians flinging themselves out of his way, creating the hole he needed to speed through to Harry.

CHAPTER 25

Floating above the masses below in Empire City, the state-of-the-art operating room in Fiske's estate hummed with activity. The surgery was fully staffed, including myriad nurses, a renowned anesthesiologist, and award-winning vascular, trauma, cardiothoracic, thoracic, and neurosurgeons—most of whom would do nothing but observe and monitor, honored to simply be there.

Archibald Moss lay on one operating table while his clone occupied the other. Both were hooked up to a blood pressure cuff, ECG leads, and a pulse oximeter. Fiske stood watching from the observation window above. English loomed beside him. Pressing a button, Fiske spoke over the intercom.

"Comfortable, Senator?"

A surgical assistant situated a plastic covering around Moss's shoulders and behind his head and began to shave off his thin strands of hair.

"I feel remorse." Moss's voice was hoarse. "Ending a new life to save my own seems . . . grotesque."

Fisk barked a laugh as the assistant produced a hand-vac and sucked up the fallen hair.

"Nonsense, Senator. The thing was grown with only a medulla oblongata. It has no *mind*. It's simpler to see it as a conveyance and you the driver. It is a commodity. No more, no less."

Moss rolled his now bald head slowly to the right and eyed the clone with surprise. The famous anesthesiologist placed a respirator over his face and the edges of his vision softened as drugs sailed into his veins.

"I will be young and beautiful," murmured Moss, reassured in his immortality, and succumbed to unconsciousness.

Fiske gazed at the scene, engrossed. As the minutes ticked by, someone cleared his throat. Fiske turned toward the silent English but spoke beyond him.

"You say you can retrieve the girl?"

Thudding footsteps rattled the observation glass as Winchester entered the room.

"Yessir, and I'll take out that Mech as a professional courtesy."

Fiske found his eyes drawn back to the operating room, the crisp white uniforms, the precise, sterile environment where amazing feats occurred, the unparalleled industry of exceptional minds. It was a comforting space, ordered and predictable, but miraculous all the same. The future of humanity, staring him in the face. And he, the master of ceremonies, would convince them of what they needed and then lead them where he wanted them to go.

"Mister English," Fiske said as an afterthought, lost in his own glory, "accompany the bounty hunter."

Mister English bowed slightly, then exited the room ahead of Winchester who lingered for a moment, eyes narrowed, watching with Fiske as the operation unfolded. Shaking his head, he followed English out, unaware that his repulsion was the height of hypocrisy.

Down in the operating arena, soft string instruments accented with sweeping piano chords flowed from the speakers. Manipulating a console, the lead neurosurgeon lowered the A-DocXI from the ceiling to hover over the senator and carefully manipulated its laser, orbiting Moss's head in a neat circle, slicing clean through down past the dura.

Next, a mechanical arm fitted with suction cups maneuvered forward from the mechanical assistant. With a pop, it pulled off the top of Moss's skull and lower layer, exposing his brain. It glistened gray and white under the meninges. On the monitor, the surgeon noted that the usual white matter lesions present in elderly brains were impressively sparse. The vascular surgeon leaned in and studied the onscreen image unblinkingly.

As the music ebbed and swelled in the background, the thoracic surgeon joined the doctors at the monitor and the neurosurgeon spoke softly to both of them. All three shook their heads subtly, their faces suffused with intellectual fascination and awe.

A subdued excitement thrummed through the air.

Fingers moving adroitly over the keyboard and controls, the neurosurgeon focused intently on the monitor where the graphic representation of Moss's brain was displayed, as performed by another arm of the A-DocXI. A stainless steel clamp braided with padding closed delicately on the senator's brain then began to back away from the skull.

It seemed as if everyone in the room stopped breathing as the machine was directed across the space between human and clone. The only audible sound was the music pumping softly in the background. The neurosurgeon tapped the keyboard, clicked a button, and rolled his finger steadily along a control, monitoring the A-DocXI as it moved into position behind the clone's prepared skull. The mechanical arm inched forward in increments, cradling its fragile bundle, and bit by bit, slowly and gently inserted Moss's brain into the skull's opening.

An almost palpable relief filled the room and the tension lightened tenfold. Everyone seemed to move at once as the music swirled grandly around them, accompanying them and the machines into the next phases of connecting blood vessels and arteries, restoring and stabilizing blood flow, and monitoring for shock.

But right now, by all appearances, it was a magnificent success.

Fiske, at the observation window, allowed himself a small, triumphant smile. He'd had no doubt everything would run smoothly but victory was still so, so sweet. As he mentally celebrated, he made a note to check with one of the auxiliary butlers that the shipwrecked bottles of Bollinger had been chilled and were ready to serve.

In the meantime, he continued to peer through the window, impressed and morbidly fascinated. *The future of humanity,* he thought, absentmindedly rolling the loose flesh of his forearm between his fingers. *Even, eventually, my own.*

CHAPTER 26

"This Buddhist walks up to a hotdog vendor and says, 'Make me one with everything.'"
–Robin Williams, *Bicentennial Man*.

Panic reigned in Jasper's operating room as the bioengineer fought for Harry's life.

Somewhere in the back of his mind, Jasper's thoughts looped over and over: *If only it was something I could see. If only it was something I could fix.* Because it could have been unstable subsystems or missed fiducial tagging or servo errors, but they were beyond all of that. They were beyond sensors and actuators and embedded firewalls and even Boolean logic.

They were somewhere Jasper had never been before with Harry, immersed in a cascade of baffling malfunctions and complex encoding glitches. He labored, second by second, breath by breath, to understand what was going on and to deliver Harry from it.

"Twenty-four point nine!" Duesenberg called out.

Jasper bent over, squinting through his magnifying glasses, and made an adjustment.

"Fifty-five point seven."

Jasper groaned. "No, too high!"

"Thirteen point three!"

Somewhere behind him, Lex sniffled softly. Jasper tore off his glasses and swiped a sleeve across his sweaty forehead. All three watched despondently as Harry's pulse zig-zagged erratically on the monitor. Thirty-eight seconds later, the electrocardiogram suddenly flatlined, flooding the room with a drawn-out tone.

Duesenberg looked at Jasper incredulously. Jasper stared down at Harry.

"He's gone." Jasper's voice wavered between disbelief and shock. "He's gone . . . "

Lex lunged between the men and grabbed Harry's face, barely able to speak. "H-Harry." Tears spilled from her eyes onto Harry's nose and lips. "Don't . . . don't give up."

***

Lex's voice echoed distantly, rapidly fading. *"Come back!"*

Deadtime was nothing the way Harry had imagined it.

Outside the shattered dome of Zumba City, light winds stirred wisps of red sand amidst the desolate landscape. The tiny white ball of the setting sun hung just above the far horizon. Harry's elongated shadow stretched across the dunes in the glowing twilight as he slowly walked toward a familiar shape.

As he came up beside it, the shape resolved into a Sentinel unit absently gazing out at the destroyed city.

"Hello, Harry," said Link from inside the machine.

"Where are we, Link?"

The armor twisted toward Harry, multiple optical lenses rotating, giving the impression that it was weighing a response.

"I think we're dead."

"Dead?" Harry contemplated his arms, his body, briefly glanced around at the fading light. "But I'm processing—"

"These are my memories. You deserve to know the whole ugly truth about what Colonel Moss did to us. Unfiltered."

The rumble of a powerful engine split the air. Harry started as an enormous shadow flowed over him. Turning slowly, he followed a huge military transport gliding through the darkening Martian sky toward the horizon. There was a sudden bedlam of noise and light, turbulence vibrating beneath his skin, like an out of body experience, and he found himself inside the ship. He revolved, unseen, amidst technicians and other military personnel, taking in his surroundings.

Ten Sentinel units were birthed in a center carousel.

Military technicians manned stations conforming to an outer ring against the bulkheads of the circular compartment. A flurry of crosstalk and activity greeted a newcomer. Colonel Moss, decades younger, vigorous, strode in with an air of command and stopped beside an aging man in a lab coat tagged Dr. Ignatius Zim who looked almost exactly like Albert Einstein.

Harry stared as his thoughts tumbled. He knew this man, this man with the snow white hair. A friend. A creator. He felt what he could only describe as love for this man, Dr. Zim.

Dr. Zim was his father.

Harry's gaze moved on, halting on a familiar figure. The figure turned its head slightly, and Harry was looking at himself. Devoid of all hair, Harry sat puppet-like before Dr. Zim who leaned over him, examining his Link implant closely with a scope. The number twenty-seven presented across the front of his unitard in stark black.

"Well," said Moss, "is it functional, Zim?"

Harry watched the scene unfold, a slow awareness blooming deep inside him, unlocking forgotten dread.

Keyboards clicked lightly in the background, interspersed with soft radio chatter. Dr. Zim straightened slowly. "The occipital interfaces are designed to modify behavior." He turned toward Moss. "Hence requiring finer adjustments." There was a heavy pause before he added grimly, "We wouldn't want to revisit the Series Six prototype incident, would we?"

Moss pushed a tight "No, indeed, we would not" through clenched teeth.

Zim faced Harry. "There. You're ready, son."

Twenty-Seven: "Thank you, Father."

Twenty-Seven stood quickly then walked woodenly toward the Battle Armor. The armor, when combined with Zim's androids, became the deadly weapons known as Sentinels—tons of lethal metal and death-dealing technology. Turning around, Twenty-Seven backed into the unit and Dr. Zim attached him with thin cables along his unitard and AI Link.

"In the event of severe damage, your occipital interface will override and return you for repairs," Dr. Zim instructed, addressing the group of Sentinels. "Take care of each other." He quickly scanned their faces. "Remember, you are all . . . one."

A chorus of android voices responded.

"We are one."

Within each of the Sentinel units on the carousel was a copy of Twenty-Seven, each assigned a different number.

Dr. Zim nodded once, briskly. "Try to obtain your mission objectives with minimal casualties. Remember, you are not killers. You are keepers of the peace."

Twenty-Seven: "We want to make you proud, Father."

Zim patted Twenty-Seven's shoulder warmly, eyes shining. "You always do."

Moss addressed the room, all business. "Seal 'em up. Prep for launch!"

Interlocking junctures of the armored units clanked closed, slowly obscuring the occupants' bodies, limb by limb, face by face, until only machine remained. Glass cylinders lowered, surrounding each unit, as Dr. Zim moved to a command station, operating a complex array of controls.

Moss vibrated with portentous energy that seemed to snake through the room, infecting the personnel with skittishness. Pacing, he spoke into a mike. "This is a priority mission. Infiltrate and secure the power station by all necessary means."

All units replied in unison: "Sir, yes, sir!"

The bottom of each cylinder on the carousel snapped open, yawning wide before a churning tornado of sanguine dust.

"Launch!"

The units were jettisoned into the roiling dust storm below.

***

Outside of Cyberwerkz, Cecil skidded the scooter recklessly through the entrance and leaped off in one movement.

"Jasper, I'm back!"

Across the garage, Duesenberg leaned around the doorway of the operating room as Jasper squeezed past and rushed out. "Come on, hurry up!" He grabbed Cecil roughly by the arm, wresting him back to the room.

"What's goin' on?"

The two of them pushed past Duesenberg. Cecil pulled the package from his messenger bag.

"Hey, Harry, I got your . . . part . . . "

The steady beep, Lex's tears, and Harry's lifeless eyes was like a punch in the face, and Cecil stammered to a stop. Jasper snatched the box out of his hand and removed the new link.

"That's impossible," Cecil said emotionally. "You're indestructible!"

The operating table whirred softly as Jasper inclined it. Moving quickly, he began to power up motorized dental instruments.

"Hand me those leads."

Cecil stood numbly, his throat working.

"We gotta get this thing outta his head, Cecil. I need you!"

Cecil snapped out of it and swung around, lunging toward a terminal on a workbench. He grabbed several wires and pulled them out. Duesenberg slumped onto a stool, hand on belly.

"This is not doing my IBS an ounce of good, no sir!" Wincing, he glanced at the monitor then did a double-take. "There's still a power reading!"

Lex and Cecil gasped. Jasper quickly brought them all back down to earth.

"It's a residual charge I'm gonna use to try'n jump-start him . . . if it ain't too late."

***

Harry watched silently, bodiless, while Vanguard Leader crouched, aiming his laser arm to cover Vanguard Three as he tore the door off the reactor hatch control.

Vanguard Leader: *"Got it?"*

A spark sizzled in a tangle of exposed wires that Vanguard Three deftly manipulated. The main hatch hissed open.

Dr. Zim and the technicians monitored the unfolding battle from the command ship. Harry remained here also, out of time, ubiquitous, experiencing multiple situations in concert. Behind them, Moss glided stealthily to a locker and silently removed a machine gun. Harry observed Moss's movements with shock. Tension escalated in his already-stressed and failing body.

Vanguard Three's voice flooded the ship's speakers: *"I'm in."*

Gunfire thundered.

Men and women screamed in surprise and terror as machine gun fire tore through them. Cables and circuits crackled as sparks showered from damaged consoles. Dr. Zim removed his headphones and locked eyes with Moss in a frozen moment. Then Moss grimaced and pulled the trigger.

Harry clenched his teeth, his fists balling impotently.

A sudden movement. Moss half-turned, gunning down a pilot emerging from the cockpit. Bullet casings clattered along the metal deck, and Moss tossed the spent weapon aside. Removing a pistol from a holster at his side, he stalked to the cockpit and disappeared inside. A flash/bang followed. Then nothing but silence.

CHAPTER 27

Acrid smoke from gunfire and shattered electronics shrouded the room as consoles hissed and popped loudly in the sudden stillness. A soft rustling revealed Zim still alive on the floor beside a table, struggling to move. He managed to pull himself sideways into a chair and lay there, twisted. Blood seeped from a wound in his chest, steadily spreading across the white lab coat.

Lying sideways in the chair, he listened to his surroundings. Then slowly and painfully he pulled himself up and faced the console on the table. He typed on the keyboard with trembling hands: Upload Keys Operation Archangel Encrypt Vngrd Ldr. As his heartbeat began to stutter and his consciousness dimmed, Zim stabbed the send button. He rolled off the chair and onto the deck, exhaling a long breath, his last thought, suffused with hope, of the Sentinels.

*****

In the Zumba City Power Station, Moss's defection speech droned on as Vanguard Leader stepped back, stunned.

"It's a trap!"

Vanguard Leader and Vanguard Three made their way ponderously to the hatch and attempted to open it.

"No good," Vanguard Three transmitted. *"We're locked in."*

Vanguard Leader swiveled, staring up at the convex containment dome.

"Not for long."

He lifted his arm and fired his laser as Vanguard Three joined in, bombarding the center of the dome with missiles discharging from shoulder pods. Inner polycarbonate panels shattered and burst as steel-reinforced concrete rumbled and violently blew apart.

"Evac!"

Firing their jump jets, Vanguard Leader and Vanguard Three rocketed through a ragged, yawning hole in the ceiling. Vanguard Three arched away, leaving a thick plume of exhaust, as Vanguard Leader landed on the remains of the dome.

"Sentinels, emergency evac!"

From different locations around the complex, broad trails of exhaust revealed the departing Sentinels soaring into the open air. A booming thunderclap that shook the sand preceded a sustained roar as the reactor detonated.

A few miles away, lifting off the sandy surface, Moss struggled to gain altitude in the command ship. A flash of light brighter than the sun erased the sky. Alarms screamed, joining the cacophony of chaos and explosions.

"Warning-warning," a computer voice announced. *"Lethal radiation levels detected. Warning-warning."*

Above Zumba City, the percussive shockwave shattered the gleaming dome, swallowing a pair of Sentinel units unable to clear the blast zone. The wave catapulted Vanguard Leader into the desert where he plowed into the sand. Behind him a black mushroom cloud expanded, turned red, then simply vanished along with the wrecked Vanguard Leader, leaving only the present Zumba City ghost town.

Link slowly turned away from the abandoned city and faced Harry.

"It was my job to ensure your optimal health," said Link. *"But I was reprogrammed to suppress your memories."* The battle armor tilted, optics roving. *"Those conflicting orders created a paradox that caused the cascade failure in my processors."*

Harry started.

"That's why you kept sabotaging me."

Images swarmed his mind's eye—Parish's rocket launcher switching to heat seeking, the missile arcing back to blow him up. Harry firing his net at Marlowe and his arm snapping to the left, sending the shot astray. The laser blast atop the junk pile in Undertown.

"I was ordered to self-destruct if there was ever a chance that you'd recover your memories," Link said. *"I had to stop you."* It seemed to pause. *"Sorry about that."*

"On whose orders?" asked Harry.

The machine faced the setting sun. It seemed like a long time before it responded. *"Colonel Moss."*

The Battle Armor began to lose substance and fade away.

"System shutdown. Harry. It's been an honor."

"Stand down, Link."

The russet Mars sands bled through the machine's vanishing body until they seemed one and the same, then it disappeared entirely, and Harry was alone. Staring out over the empty plain, Harry faced the phantom Martian landscape, suffused with a profound sense of stillness. He stood before the dead city, the desert, and the setting sun, no longer able to sense the boundary between himself and his surroundings. Suspended in the center of an unassailable calm for the first time ever, he realized all thought had been extinguished. The voice was gone. His being was empty. His mind moved to Jasper: *Was this what he'd meant by empty mind? Was this emptiness?*

Emptiness . . .

CHAPTER 28

Jasper worked frantically on the old link unit as Cecil handed him a tiny tool.

"Seven millimeter!" Cecil affirmed.

"That's a six. I thought you could actually see with those big-ass eyes!"

Duesenberg made a sound between a cough and a groan. "The residual charge is fading!"

Lex pressed against the wall, hugging herself.

"Okay, I'm almost ready." Jasper jerked his head toward Cecil. "Hand me the new one!" Turning back, he eased out the old link and handed it to Cecil, then eased in the new one as Duesenberg joined Lex against the wall.

Jasper quickly attached leads from a nearby device to the new link and then depressed a button. Harry convulsed violently and fell back, dead. Sweat ran in rivulets down Jasper's face as he hit the button again, to no avail. Duesenberg met Jasper's eyes and slowly shook his head. Disbelief flooded the room. Duesenberg laid a gentle hand on Lex's shoulder. Jasper slammed his fist against the cart and adjusted the controls, firing again, this time for a long hit. Harry's body spasmed violently. Cecil inhaled and Duesenberg flinched, and Harry collapsed again into stillness.

Everyone looked around the room, dazed. The tableau lingered, moored in denial. The force of the emotion caught all by surprise, though in different measures, a naked sensation of loss and waste, the idea that someone had affected their lives so irrefutably that their existence would now be less somehow, and wanting. They didn't want Harry to just stay alive. They wanted Harry to be present in their lives, and they in his. He possessed a uniqueness that was missing in the everyday, almost like the magic of old that people no longer believed in.

The repudiation unfurled and extended. If no one spoke, if it wasn't cemented in words, it wouldn't be official. There was still possibility, there was still hope. But as the silence encroached, slowly weighing them down, and Harry's eyes remained sightless and the monitors told them no different from what they were seeing, they began to succumb. Their shoulders dropped, their faces slackened. They moved listlessly, still not speaking, but now out of resignation rather than hope, and prepared to leave the room.

As Jasper and Cecil bent to their tasks and Duesenberg and Lex stood awkwardly by, a beep sounded. Then another. Everyone stopped. Jasper whirled, studying the monitor. "Pulse!" he shouted over the beeps as the others waited, unsure. He punched the air as the reading picked up speed and strength. "We've got a pulse!"

An explosive sigh burst from three sets of lungs along with shouts and astonished laughter. Lex hugged Duesenberg and Jasper immediately began to tweak the new link as Cecil watched over his shoulder. Cecil glanced toward the monitor, then away. Then he looked back.

"What's this?"

A shield and sword had appeared on the screen, overlaid by the word Vanguard in bold letters. After several seconds, the Vanguard logo disappeared, replaced by scrolling numbers and encrypted code.

"Harry's operating system's reloading." Jasper pushed his magnifying glasses up and frowned. "Vanguard?"

Duesenberg shouldered his way between them. "Those old Sentinel units. That was their call sign, right?"

Cecil whispered, looking awestruck, "Strategic Command Shadow Ops . . . "

Lex pushed between the men huddled around the computer as Harry stirred on the operating table. "Shadow what?"

For a moment, no one spoke.

"Buddha's golden ass!" Cecil yelled. "The Butchers of Zumba!"

Jasper rounded on him. "Don't blaspheme in my shop!"

"I'm an anarchist, man."

"Great Tathagata," Jasper breathed, staring at the screen. "50,000 lives wiped out."

Lex squinted at the computer as if that would help her understand it better. Behind them, Harry stiffly sat up, removed the leads from the back of his head, plucked the transceiver from his ear, and quietly set it down beside him.

"He's a weapon of mass destruction!" Cecil whisper/screamed, still facing the monitor.

"Quick, shut him down!" Duesenberg glanced behind him. His face fell. "Um . . . never mind."

Cecil and Jasper spun around and cringed. In perfect synchronization, all three men began to back out of the operating room.

Watching them, Lex said, "Why are you guys acting so funny?"

Jasper jumped forward and grabbed Lex, yanking her away from Harry as he climbed off the table and casually switched off the monitor.

"That's classified," he said in a dangerous voice.

"H-Harry . . . " Jasper was trembling. "N-now, t-take it easy."

"Yeah, we fixed your Vanguard—weapon—BRAIN!" Cecil sputtered.

The men bounced off each other in their hurry to back away as Harry absently compressed the gaping coveralls closed that Jasper had torn open earlier. Duesenberg looked haunted, as if gazing up at the underside of a pitted pachyderm hoof aimed for his head. Harry silently followed them out into the shop.

Suddenly, Harry cocked his head toward the front door then advanced on them menacingly, corralling them against the wall. The men cried out in terror and Lex closed her eyes and covered her ears.

An explosion like twenty bombs going off rocked the building and everyone screamed as Jasper's van smashed through the ceiling. The front door exploded, flooding the entryway with smoke, and thudding footsteps vibrated through the floor until Winchester was standing before them. Mister English followed, wearing a rocket pack.

"Knock, knock," Winchester's voice rumbled.

Jasper and Cecil ogled the giant cowboy.

"Leonard Little?" they said together.

Winchester bristled and started to respond, then shook it off.

"We're here for the girl," he announced.

"Jasper," said Harry, "where's my Enforcer?"

"You mean the rifle?"

"Yes."

"It's in the van."

They both turned and stared at Jasper's pancaked van lying in the middle of the shop, ticking and hissing. Lex squirmed away from Jasper and placed herself between the two groups.

"Stop." She looked at Harry. "I won't let you suffer because of me." A bittersweet expression crossed her face. "Nobody should suffer over some old memory."

Harry stepped toward her.

"Harry, you're fired!"

Harry stopped cold and watched her tensely, noting Winchester raising his Enforcer in his peripheral vision. His attention shifted to Mister English when he moved forward and grabbed Lex. She stood rigidly, not resisting. With Winchester's rifle aimed in their general direction, nobody moved a muscle as English attached Lex to his harness, gripped the rocket pack's controls, and ignited the engines.

"Thanks for everything, Harry." Lex raised her voice over the rumbling engines, her eyes brimming. English lifted up, angled toward the hole, and flew into the night sky. Winchester made good their escape, then turned back to the group.

"That's half the job done," he rumbled impassively. "Now I'm gonna kill ya, Harry. Nothin' personal." He reached up and tilted his hat back and made a moue. "Well, maybe a little bit personal."

"Uh . . . that's our cue, fellas." Cecil telescoped his arms and latched onto a roof girder. Legs whirring and clicking as they extended, he roped Jasper and Duesenberg and hauled them upward with him.

Jasper started. "Cecil!" He squirmed around, glaring up at his adopted son. Duesenberg gripped his stomach with both hands as he endured the ignoble departure.

"Good luck, Leonard," came Cecil's voice from somewhere above, snickering. "You're gonna need it."

Winchester took two lumbering steps forward.

"You have no idea how humiliatin' it was doin' all the footwork while you had all the fun." His expression was decidedly less than friendly.

Harry stood still, poker-faced.

"I was like a flower growin' in the shadow of a tree," Winchester continued his one-man pity party. "Now *I'm* the tree!" he thundered dramatically.

He stepped forward again, irked to receive no response, physical or otherwise, from his former partner.

"Do you remember," he started in a low, threatening voice, "that you picked me up . . . " His voice began to rise. "And tossed me across the room?" Now he was shouting. "Do you know how degradin' that was?!"

Without waiting for a response, he rapid fired in Harry's direction. The bullets pinged and ricocheted across empty air. Startled, he swung around to find Harry standing beside him.

"Wha—"

"You must weigh as much as a tree in *that* getup," Harry mused.

Winchester's gigantic arm shot out in a devastating haymaker. Harry ducked and watched as Winchester spun around, off balance.

"You went for armor instead of agility and speed. Thought I trained you better . . . Little."

"I ain't Little!"

Winchester hoisted the rifle and Harry dipped into a backbend, kicking off Winchester's chest and knocking him cockeyed. He hand walked backwards then bounced to his feet and flexed his fingers, impressed.

"Looks like you got upgrades," said Winchester. Two panels across his chest flipped open, tearing his shirt apart and revealing multiple missile warheads. "Me too."

The missiles fired and detonated directly on top of Harry. The operating suite was blown asunder, plaster and wood and concrete flying in every direction. Outside, back on the ground, Duesenberg and Cecil peered through a window and flinched. Jasper cupped his cheeks.

"They're blowin' my place apart!"

Duesenberg faced him sternly. "You take out the insurance I told you about?"

Jasper wilted. "No."

Cecil patted him consolingly on the shoulder. "Bummer."

In the shattered remnants of the shop, Winchester grinned arrogantly through the swirling smoke and scattering debris. Harry was gone. He couldn't even see the parts. The missiles had simply disintegrated him. Satisfied, he began to lower his weapon and secure his formidable chest cavity in preparation to depart.

"Well, that explains the weight." Harry's disembodied voice floated down from above.

Winchester's head snapped up, his grin vanishing. Harry sat casually on the edge of the demolished roof. He dropped down lightly.

"M-one surefire TACs. Heavy," said Harry.

Face contorted, Winchester barreled forward like a train, gaining speed as Harry performed a neat cartwheel, moving toward the back of the shop. Unable to stop his momentum, Winchester smashed through a wall, slipped and skidded into the metal shield partition, smacking his head with a clank.

Harry watched. "Very heavy," he commented. "You oughta get into demolition. You'd make a great bulldozer."

Winchester blundered to his feet and threw another wild set of uncontrolled punches. "I'll bulldoze *you!*"

The compromised structure creaked ominously and something metallic clinked to the floor. Harry backed into the scanner room and Winchester eagerly followed, his face bloated with rage and battered pride. Finding Harry leaning against the scanner, Winchester swung his rifle up and aimed it at point blank range.

"You think Mechs go to heaven, Harry?"

"All conscious beings go to heaven."

"Send me a postcard."

Winchester rapid fired in a tight arc, bullets tearing through the air, missing Harry by a hair's breadth, as he switched on the scanner then breezily executed a somersault over the partition, nailing the landing with ease.

Winchester stopped firing. "Uh-oh."

Light strobed, painting the top of the wall. Circuits sparked and transistors ignited as Winchester's electrical network burned.

Harry ambled into the room. Electrical arcs danced across Winchester's body and blue smoke flowed from around his neck. He teetered, seemingly on the verge of regaining his stability, but then abruptly plunged backward, smashing the scanner flat with a resounding crash.

Harry picked up Winchester's rifle.

"I'm gonna borrow your Enforcer."

Winchester stared up at him from the floor. His demeanor had improved greatly. "Sure thing, Harry."

"And your ride."

"Top left pocket."

Amid the sound of Winchester's internal drives spinning down, Harry reached under his duster and removed a fob.

"Shielding, Leonard. Look into it."

"Sound advice." Winchester gazed up at Harry from the floor. "Maybe if I had shieldin', things mighta turned out different, huh, Harry?"

Harry slung the Enforcer across his back and pocketed the fob. He looked down at Winchester. "That's right. I would've had to kill you, Leonard." He turned and strode past Jasper and Duesenberg as they rushed into the room.

"Where're you going?" Jasper threw his arms out.

"She's my client."

"Wait a minute," Duesenberg reminded him. "She fired you, remember?"

Harry kept walking, not responding.

Jasper approached Winchester who lay frozen amid the scanner wreckage and sat, friendly-like, on his chest.

"You fried every servo and relay in your *very* expensive body, Leonard." He drummed his fingers on Winchester's body pensively. "It's gonna cost a fortune to get my place fixed and you up and runnin'."

"Top right pocket."

Jasper fished out a PDA, tapped several buttons, then broke out into a brilliant smile.

"Oh, yeah, that'll cover it."

Near the front door, Harry was pulling on his visor as he pushed past Cecil on his way out of the shop.

"That was totally awesome!" Cecil yelled after him, knowing they had all thought they were going to die a minute ago, but not caring. Because now this new, incredible thing had happened. Harry was turning out to be something else. More than unique even. Something amazing.

CHAPTER 29

"Every love story is a ghost story."
–David Foster Wallace

Dr. Oliver Rosewood paced anxiously, wearing a hole in the luxurious carpet of Moss's armored passenger cabin. For the eighth or ninth time, he bent over the hatch and looked for a way to force it open but then backed off, his mind awhirl. His instinct was to get out and find Lex, but then images of the tank, of his daughter struggling to stay afloat, flooded his mind like the drowning waters that had likely ended her life, and the pain and remorse were unbearable.

Not again. Not her.

Breathing hard, Dr. Rosewood braced himself against the wall.

Not again. Not Lex. And then he thought: *I won't survive this.*

A door opened in his mind, and, powerless to stop, he found himself turning and stepping through without hesitation.

***

It was late fall on the Georgetown University campus, thirty years ago, and the bronze Autumn Cherry leaves glowed brilliant red and gold in the sun. Oliver was buying a coffee at GroundedV when he realized he'd left his wallet in his apartment. As he patted himself down for the third time and the cashier's business-like smile became strained, someone chuckled and tapped him on the shoulder and said, "My treat."

Turning around, Oliver experienced the first and last "movie moment" that he would ever have when the coffee and the cashier and the walls and the school and the world and all of time vanished as if they had never been there, leaving only Eleanor standing before him, a ray of sunlight painting her black hair silver.

Soon known to their friends and family as the Odd Couple, they fell deeply in love, the sublime embodiment of "opposites attract." Artistic, extroverted Eleanor consumed and disseminated music and dance and laughter while quiet science nerd Oliver brushed aside the world's veil, revealing the beauty of faraway stars and planets or making theories like the uncertainty principle sound riveting and exciting. Gently excavating each other's passions, they uncovered the burning embers that powered the synergy of their lives.

Having finished medical school, Oliver pursued his PhD while Eleanor completed her BFA in music. He then later moved into genetics while an orchestra hired Eleanor for a rare, coveted pianist position. Nuptials followed with a house soon after. Their lives continued seamlessly toward what seemed like an endlessly bright and promising future.

∗∗∗

Five years later, when the Kāne Event occurred, it only strengthened their bond. Life changed for them in many ways, like everyone else, but the core of Oliver and Eleanor remained unwavering. Oliver began a business, Rosewood Biomedical Company, and Eleanor was fascinated by his work—growing organs for those who needed them, affording them a second chance at life. For himself, Oliver enjoyed nothing more than watching his wife's hands fly up and down a keyboard, loose strands of black hair leaping around her face as she pounded out the chords. He built a lab in their basement so that he could pursue his interests in his spare time, and they bought a used Baby Grand and stationed it proudly in the living room.

When Eleanor began to randomly miss notes at the piano, she at first attributed it to exhaustion. Her orchestra had gone on a mini goodwill tour across the South to raise money for those areas closer to and therefore harder hit by the Kāne Event. But months later, she was still missing notes, and more often. Worse, now she would return home from doing any of her usual errands completely exhausted, needing to sleep until the next day. Soon after, tripping and stumbling became a worrisome addition on top of everything else.

Oliver's concern deepened into panic which he folded away out of her view but kept close at hand. Forcing her to finally see a specialist, an exam resulted in nothing either of them were expecting or wanted to hear: a diagnosis of Amyotrophic Lateral Sclerosis, a neurological disease affecting motor neurons. The diagnosis also made it abruptly clear why they'd never gotten pregnant. But although the news wasn't good, the couple was strong. Surely they hadn't survived the Event just to succumb to this. They vowed to fight.

The fight, however, would be short.

Oliver watched as the light of his life, of his very universe, began to fade like a flickering candle. Within weeks of the diagnosis, all piano playing had ceased. Music fled their house, though Eleanor somehow remained light and determined. For what, Oliver didn't know, because there was no cure, but he was humbled by her indomitable nature. She tried to make him laugh, and he laughed and laughed, returning the effort the best he could, gratified to see her smile and hear her soft giggles. When she was asleep, he alternately sobbed or turned to stone.

Every other waking moment Oliver spent in his lab in the basement, obsessed with finding a cure.

The decline was rapid. Oliver fought to stay ahead of it. All else in his life was thrown aside—his company, his employees. Nothing else mattered. When Eleanor's speech began to slur, his innards liquefied. When she acquired a limp, ice coated his veins. He lost all sense of taste and no longer knew what day it was. Suddenly it was obvious she needed a walker. Five weeks later, it had escalated to a wheelchair. He wiped her mouth tenderly at meals and read to her until she fell asleep.

"Hey, Mr. Organ Man," Eleanor would slur playfully, "why don't you grow me a new body?" making him smile and respond, "Are you kidding? I am! It'll be ready in a week." They'd both chuckle, intent on lifting the other one's spirits while diligently ignoring the irony.

He worked nonstop, barely sleeping or eating. The time came when she had to be moved to hospice, and he tripled his efforts, almost killing himself in the process. Failing at a cure, he settled instead for scrubbing the disease from her DNA. But as he sensed the end approaching, he abandoned the work to stay with her day and night.

He was holding her hand one Saturday morning, staring at the wall, when she exhaled and didn't inhale again. He laid his head against her breastbone and closed his eyes. Outside, snowflakes swirled gently out of a steel-gray sky.

Oliver's plunge into depression was even worse than his obsessive journey to save his wife. Eleanor hadn't been in the house for months, but now that she was no longer in the world he felt the difference acutely. He fumed at the universe taunting him with her DNA, finally disease-free, but no longer having *her*. Grief and frustration denuded his soul as he wandered through his empty home like an apparition, consumed by woe.

Then one night, he sat up on the sofa where he'd slumped into unconsciousness, his eyes wide in the darkness as Eleanor's voice echoed in his mind: *Why don't you grow me a new body?*

Although growing organs wasn't against the law, cloning human beings was.

Oliver didn't care.

His heart clamored with insurrection as the potential unfolded before him.

Though combining his DNA with his wife's wasn't true cloning, the process would nevertheless still be reviled and probably terminated so, electrified, elated, he undertook the process downstairs in his lab, then began to grow the baby in an artificial womb. He monitored in amazement, tracking each development with mounting excitement, counting down the months, hours, and seconds when the child would join the world. With his joie de vivre revitalized, he turned toward getting his life back on track. He reopened Rosewood Biomedical and began to regain his footing in the market.

And then the baby *was* in the world, cradled in Oliver's arms. Time passed joyfully as he raised his secret miracle child. His daughter lightened all the dark corners and electrified his purpose, and he flooded her world with love.

One day at work, associates of Fiske contacted him for an order of tailor-made lungs, minus the small cell cancer that had ravaged the originals, and Oliver did not disappoint. Thus began a relationship which would lead to Fiske himself inquiring, years later, "What else can you do with this technology?"

Hindsight was 20/20, as they say, because otherwise Oliver would have kept his mouth shut. He would have never revealed the truth about how his daughter had come to be, and Fiske would not have invited him to do it again. Not the traditional way, though. Rapidly and unnaturally, by implementing Fiske's Mutagen X.

But the damage had been done. Fiske knew his secret and he made the offer. Intrigued initially, Oliver would ultimately refuse when he discovered he would be cloning Colonel Moss. He would not clone the person who had abandoned Earth, along with the People's Republic of Mars. But of course, in the end, once one has opened the door to vampires, one couldn't stop them from coming in and doing what they did best. At that point, it was already too late.

***

In the cabin, Dr. Rosewood backed out of the room in his mind and closed the door. The memories had raced by, the past unspooling before him in seconds, and he recognized the pool of despair trying to draw him under. No. He wouldn't submit. Eleanor would not have given in. Regardless of what he'd witnessed, the rising water covering Lex, there was a possibility that she had survived. *She could still be alive.*

Rosewood turned around, catching sight of himself in a small mirror on the wall, his still-swollen mouth and tortured eyes. A clenching pain coiled behind his ribs. Then he found himself standing before the hatch again, looking for a way to force it open, his mind caught in a tortured battle between possibility and probability.

Suddenly there was a click, the hatch clanged open, and the sweetest voice he had ever heard in his life shot straight into his brain.

"Let go of me, oaf!"

CHAPTER 30

English shoved Lex roughly and she stumbled into the room. He yanked the vault-like hatch shut behind her with ease, the metallic clank ringing loudly. Rosewood stood stock still, afraid he was hallucinating.

Then, "Alexia!" burst hoarsely from his throat.

Alive. She's alive alive alive.

Lex straightened up, eyes wide. "Dad!"

They rushed together and embraced. Rosewood murmured, "Alexia, Alexia . . . I thought the worst," while Lex clung to him and swallowed hard, refusing to cry anymore today. Rosewood held her tightly, crushing his fear away, terrible desperation morphing into an exquisite relief and helpless, piercing love.

Suddenly Lex stiffened, remembering something. She pulled away, wound up, and slapped her father. Rosewood winced and grabbed his cheek. At least it was the uninjured side of his face.

"Alexia Eleanor Rosewood!"

"Don't you Alexia Eleanor Rosewood me! You cloned me from your dead wife!" she screamed with the kind of fury only teenaged girls possessed. "What am I, a science project?!" Lex turned and flung herself into the recliner and covered her face with her arms.

"Alexia." Rosewood faced her. "You're not a clone of your mother!"

"She wasn't my *mother*," she hissed, "she was an *organ donor!*"

Alexia sank further into the chair, miserable. Dorcas wouldn't believe it when she told her. Would she even want to be her friend still? Maybe she shouldn't tell her. She couldn't tell anyone, ever, her entire life.

Rosewood waited while Lex fumed, every cell of his body still swooning with joy at the sight of her.

He approached his daughter as she huddled in the ridiculous recliner upholstered with pitiful imitation skins, lowered himself to one knee, and took her hand. She tried to yank it away but he held fast. He waited until she calmed down then tilted his head, trying to make eye contact. She refused to look at him.

"You have no idea," he murmured so softly that she found herself listing slightly closer, "what she was like, your mother." Rosewood closed his eyes. "I should have talked about her more. I should have told you everything about her."

Lex turned toward him. He opened his eyes.

"What she endured . . . was horrible. What we . . . " He stopped. His mouth was dry. He swallowed. "I couldn't save her." He lowered his head as tears beaded his lashes. Without hesitation, Lex grabbed both of his hands. "I realized later . . . " He sniffled and looked up at her. "That *you* were in there. *You* were waiting." Now Lex was sniffling along with him. "My love compelled me to make certain this cold world wouldn't be denied the warmth of that spirit. That light. That light waiting in *you*." He laughed softly. "Whatever my genes contributed pales in comparison to the strength of that spirit . . . " He gave her a tremulous smile. "Your mother's strength humbled me. And now so does yours. So here I am, humbled again."

Lex sat up. "*Your* genes . . . ?"

Rosewood nodded, running a hand tiredly across his face. Lex leaned into him emotionally, and he wrapped his arms around her. "You mean I'm a real person?" she whispered into his shoulder, and he squeezed her tightly. "Of course you're real. You're *my daughter.* Genetic or otherwise."

Tears poured down Lex's cheeks and she happily let them. She and her father embraced for a long time, clinging to one another, mentally spent but also profoundly heartened.

"I'm sorry." Lex sniffled and pulled back, scrutinizing his lip. "I'm sorry I slapped you."

Rosewood ran a tender thumb over her discolored cheek, looked like he was going to say something, then cleared his throat. "You're here. You're alive. You're okay." He started to stand up. "You're my daughter. But you're so like your mother. Her passion, her beauty . . . "

He straightened and dusted invisible particles off his slacks. "Seems all you inherited from me was your blond hair—"

He stared at her, confused. Belatedly, the black, spiky hair, now somewhat bedraggled from the water, filled his vision until it was the only thing he could see. The fading black lips and eyeliner followed shortly.

"Are you wearing makeup, young lady?" He paused. "And why aren't you in school?"

Lex started. She leaped out of the recliner.

"Man, I'm starving!" she said, trying to drum up some sympathy— fast. "Is there anything to eat around here?" She gazed around the cabin, taking everything in. Rushing to the cabinets, she threw them open one by one, finding them as empty as her stomach.

Rosewood watched her, smiling at her transparent attempt at misdirection. Lex threw her arms out.

"Was I morbidly obese in another life? What's with this karma?!"

She continued looking through the compartment, searching for a forgotten box of crackers or even a jar of Petra's Naked Soya Butter.

Finding both would have been heaven. Instead, she noticed the walls were lined with handicap handholds, and she immediately moved between them, yanking on each one until one of them wobbled.

"Gimme a hand, Dad."

"What are you doing?"

She grinned unpleasantly. "When that ape comes back, he's in for a surprise."

Rosewood joined Lex at the wall and they heaved on the handle together.

CHAPTER 31

Moss's clone opened his eyes.

He was lying in bed in a softly-lit room with no windows, two other beds (empty), and a huge viewing screen in one corner near the ceiling, turned off.

Immediately, he tried to sit up but could not. His head was immobilized somehow, his thoughts foggy. Raising a hand to try to locate the restraints, he stopped mid-movement. The hand he was looking at was not his own. It was young, unlined, unblemished. He raised the other hand, trembling, and held them side by side. This taut skin, this plump, obscenely glowing luster was his. These *were* his hands, from forty years ago. Science had plundered time itself and delivered back to him what should have been lost in this life forever.

The clone's arms dropped back to the bed and he exhaled shakily. He'd done it. He'd actually done it. He'd lived most of his years already, but now he had an entirely new life stretching out ahead of him, burning with affirmation, the contract rewritten. He could barely wrap his mind around it. Triumph roared in his ears.

His fingers scrabbled along the bed on either side of him, the left hand encountering what he was looking for—the call button. As he shifted to press it, a nurse entered the room, followed by Fiske and Mister English.

Fiske was brisk and straight forward. "Ah, Senator. How are we feeling?"

"*I'm* feeling fine," the Moss clone snapped. He zeroed in on the nurse with barely contained excitement. "I can't move my head." His eyes raced around the room as if searching for something. "Adjust these restraints. And bring me a mirror."

The nurse hurriedly released the clone from the rigid head support attached to the bed. The cervical thoracic head and spine brace, affixed over his clavicle, down his chest, around his back, and molded snugly beneath his chin, remained. The clone attempted to move his head, testing mobility (there was none) as Fiske and Mister English observed from a polite distance. Obnoxiously snapping his fingers, the Moss clone barked, "The mirror! Bring me the mirror!"

"Now, Senator—" began Fiske, and the clone cut him off.

"How long do I have to wear this ridiculous contraption?" He gestured at the brace as the nurse stepped on a floor pedal, carefully raising the bed, then handed him a mirror.

"I'm afraid all the way back to Mars, Senator," Fiske informed him.

"Then let's start that journey. Take me to the Spaceport!"

"Senator, we need to run tests. You shouldn't be moved—"

"I'm not asking, Fiske. And I'm altering the deal. I'm taking the doctor and the girl with me."

Fiske began to respond but thought better of it. There was no point in arguing with the senator over minor divergences. Still, displeased, he turned to Mister English and cleared his throat. "Mister English, set course for Poughkeepsie Spaceport."

Mister English bowed and left as Moss's clone stared into the mirror, touching his face, enraptured.

✳✳✳

Mister English made his way dutifully through the Fiske estate, his rubber soles squeaking on the polished marble floors. A sudden hush preceded his arrival as maids, assistants, and various others parted like the Red Sea. As usual, Mister English said nothing and acknowledged no one, which was more than fine with all present.

On his way through the hallway with the creamy yellow lighting, he paused to gently straighten Moksha's uncrooked frame and stood back to read the wise woman's aphorism as he did every day. To Mister English, it said nothing and everything at the same time. He didn't possess the exact words or understanding, but to him it perfectly mirrored the human condition.

The hangar buzzed with the business of the day as Mister English entered and ascended to one of the control room stations. Focused on crucial duties, no one in the hangar noticed Fiske's valet or stopped what they were doing in acknowledgement of his presence. Mister English didn't care, either way. As long as everyone was doing their job.

The valet manipulated the controls deftly, and the estate's engines revved as it began to climb above the Empire City skyline and higher into the clouds. As he checked the trim and punched in coordinates, an urgent beeping suddenly shrilled. The screen before him snapped on, revealing an image of Winchester's aerolite whisking through the growing dawn in what appeared to be hot pursuit.

Mister English cocked his head to the side, grudgingly impressed.

He hadn't thought Winchester would be able to dispense with that other Mech, the troublesome one, so quickly. He found himself assigning mental kudos to the giant cowboy. But he wasn't sure what he was doing here, now. As an afterthought, he zoomed in on the cockpit, and Harry's visored face stared back at him.

***

Fiske was seated at the gigantic marble table in the meeting hall, still compartmentalizing the irritation and concern Moss's clone had stirred up with his unexpected demands and forcing a change in their schedule. He pored over financial readouts, his lips moving silently as he studied the data, not even noticing when the former Chef Robuchon slipped into the room and refilled his empty cup with Da Hong Pao tea.

Ordinarily exorbitant, the tea had gone down in price recently, and Chef Robuchon had made it her mission to secure a pound of it between her duties in the laundry room and aiding with scullery work. Due to these efforts, she'd been promoted back to the kitchen, but only as a server and sometimes dish washer. It didn't matter to her. She was determined to reclaim her previous lofty position as Head Chef, no matter what it took, and she was already on her way.

As Chef Robuchon completed the pour and exited the room with a bounce in her step, Mister English's face appeared on the window video screen, interrupting the stock market ticker.

Fiske glanced up.

"Trouble, Mister English?"

The screen switched from Mister English to Harry. Fiske pounded the table, sending the cup of Da Hong Pao flying.

"It's alive?! Incinerate it!"

The tea soaked into his papers and spilled across a Holotab. Fiske beat on the table again.

"WHO PUT THIS TEA HERE? COME BACK HERE AT ONCE!"

Outside the door of the meeting hall, Chef Robuchon froze and then began to tiptoe away like a character in a cartoon. Still trembling from the fury in Fiske's voice, she found herself thinking of her former teacher, a Kenyan Chef de Cuisine who had been fond of often quoting, "A snake you can see does not bite."

With sudden clarity, Chef Robuchon understood that that simply wasn't true, and, sadly, she saw herself as if from a distance, channeling all of her energy and ambition into what amounted to an unstable and toxic environment. But she was even sadder to realize that her former mentor was a pompous moron. And so what did that make her?

⁂

In the hangar, Mister English was already busy locking crosshairs. An acquisition signal whined, and he pressed a big red fire button.

"*Missile away,*" the computer voice droned. Mister English crossed his arms and focused on the screen.

In Winchester's aerolite, Harry watched a red dot appear on his visor and immediately began evasive maneuvers. The aerolite banked left sharply and plunged down through the clouds as the missile closed in. Angling into a steep dive, Harry lifted his visor and located the tailgating missile in the side view mirrors. He Mech-handled the controls, and the vehicle looped over in a tight arc and blasted upward. The missile mirrored the maneuvers and closed in.

Bursting through the clouds, the aerolite raced straight for the estate.

Harry aimed Winchester's van at one of the estate's rear engines, pulling up at the last second. The missile continued straight ahead. The hangar rocked violently with the concussion and workers stumbled and cried out. Without missing a beat, English locked on the aerolite and fired again.

"Missile away."

The second missile blasted from beneath the estate and instantly locked on.

Harry maneuvered the vehicle deftly, but this time the projectile was tracking tightly and quickly gaining ground. Harry engaged the autopilot and slung his rifle. He slid the sunroof open and pulled himself up.

Fighting gale force winds, Harry gauged approaching death. He counted steadily in a whisper then jumped. The missile connected, annihilating the aerolite. The shockwave launched Harry across open sky toward a maintenance catwalk ringing the estate platform. He flipped over the railing smoothly, just in time to see the flaming, spinning aerolite wreckage pierce the clouds below.

Alarms blasted, seemingly coming from everywhere at once.

In the hangar, Mister English stalked toward the stairs and stomped upward, shouldering a technician over the banister with impunity. His short cry rang out as the remaining workers hustled clear of the approaching behemoth of a valet. Mister English reached a heavy hatch, spun the wheel, annoyed, with one hand, and flung the thick metal portal open as if it was made of feathers.

Outside, Harry strained against buffeting winds. Seeing Mister English, he unslung his rifle and fired a net that swaddled the valet tightly. English smirked and tore through it like it was string. Flipping a switch on the rifle, Harry fired twice in rapid succession. Almost casually, Mister English's hands shot out, catching a pair of smoke grenades. He then crushed them, staring daggers at Harry as he did, and flung them over the side.

Flipping the switch again, Harry rapid fired bullets, turning English's neat white shirt and stylish waistcoat into Swiss cheese. English smirked some more, glanced unconcernedly at his shredded clothing, then tore them the rest of the way off, revealing a powerful metal chassis and extenuating arms with monstrous hydraulic actuators, comically topped by relatively small hands covered with demure beige gloves.

Harry slung his rifle and burst forward, leaping into a flying kick. He bounced off of English's chest like a rubber ball. English snatched Harry's spinning legs, hauled him up, and threw him over the side.

Snagging the underside of the catwalk, Harry's body swayed over empty sky below. Loud thudding shook the metal as English tried to stomp on his fingers, a millisecond too late, as Harry shimmied away. Harry flipped back over the railing and broke for the hatch full speed, the valet on his tail. Grabbing an overhead pipe, he executed a full revolution, slamming English in the back as he swung around behind him.

English careened toward the mid-port engine.

Harry leapt onto his back and grabbed his throat, barely able to grip the thick column of muscle. English reached back, plucked Harry off one-handed, and effortlessly pounded him onto the catwalk. He immediately yanked him up again and slammed his pelvis with a powerful blow, sending a shock through Harry's accelerometers and micro-gyro stabilizers.

Harry collapsed.

Gripping the railing, English ripped it apart then brandished it like a club and battered Harry repeatedly. Harry kicked out blindly, hoping the valet's crotch wasn't armored as well. His foot walloped the target and English wobbled back, cupping his privates. A plaintive howl spiraled upward, competing with the thrumming engines. Harry surged to his feet and dove at the compromised juggernaut. They both tumbled over the side, plummeting toward the engine's maw. Catching the lip of the catwalk, English's body swung out, and Harry slid down behind him, latching onto his legs.

Dangerously close to the engine's swirling turbine, Harry strained against the downward suction. He began to inch himself up over English as their combined weight stressed the trestle's lip, tearing a crevice in the metal. Once atop the catwalk, Harry immediately reached for the valet, seizing his hand as the metal snapped off. English turned away from the thrumming engine and looked up at Harry, resigned to his doom.

"As we are . . . "

His lips moved, but Harry couldn't hear him. He focused on his faltering grip. Leaning over as far as possible, he slapped his other hand down on top of the valet's, straining.

"So it goes . . . "

Mister English's glove peeled off and he dropped like a stone, plunging feet-first into the engine. The explosive concussion pitched Harry sideways into the railing, hard enough to snap ribs if he'd had any. He recovered quickly, located the hatch, and entered the hangar.

CHAPTER 32

Hearing the distant explosion, Fiske struggled upright behind the meeting hall table, gripping the slick, tea-covered surface as the room began to slowly tilt. The screen on the wall showed a shiny-faced control room technician checking readings across a series of panels in a near panic.

"The reactors are overloading!"

Behind the technician, chaos reigned.

"Where's Mister English?" Fiske found himself shouting.

"Sir, we've lost two port engines. We can't maintain altitude!"

One of the panels exploded, showering the technician with fractured shards.

"Raise reactor output!" Fiske pressed his fists into the table to steady himself as the room shook violently.

"We have to abandon the estate!" the tech yelled, and ran out of view.

As Fiske opened his mouth to scream at the tech, the meeting hall listed sharply to one side and his father's marble table grated over the floor, pressing into Fiske's belly and pinning him against the window/screen.

"Mister English . . . " Unable to get air into his compressed lungs, he could only whisper. "Help me . . . "

He had been sipping tea one moment and reviewing reports and numbers, and now he couldn't breathe. How had this happened? He was the man who never had time for himself, never had time to relax, always working, always building a better tomorrow. He had facilitated a successful brain transfer operation into a clone!

The road to immortality lay ahead, a fresh, unspoiled virgin path, leading into yet-unknown wealth and frontiers . . . so how was this happening? He didn't have time to be pinned by this ridiculous table, and he didn't have time to die, and Mister English, for the first time ever, was being unforgivably derelict in his duties.

Turning his head, he had a perfect view of the ground approaching through the window, framed exquisitely, like a photograph, like a movie, and he didn't feel the impulse to scream for many long moments, because his mind would not accept what was happening.

Instead, he saw fields of golden wheat stretching out for miles, bending and turning. He could feel the light wind, and the sun was shining as never before, orange and yellow, warm and comforting. He thought for a moment, *is this the future?* Because the future was his, and it lay in his palm, the miracle of accelerated growth and food for everyone and immortality for a chosen few.

Because he *did* want to change the world and he knew he could help, but he wielded the power, which must be acknowledged, because nothing came free. Not assistance. Not favors. Not food.

Not life.

Suddenly Fiske snapped back, seeing the approaching earth anew. He realized the fields of wheat he had seen in his mind's eye had been something else, not the future. For a brief moment he decided, *that was my childhood.* But then that was quickly discarded, too, because there had been no fields of wheat or shining sun in his past. His childhood had transpired in a dark room on his father's lap, surrounded by strangers, sweet joy and the lull of adult conversation interspersed with impotent rage in a repeating loop.

But the wheat, the fields of shining wheat bending in the wind beneath the golden sun— he remembered now. It had been a photograph of his grandfather as a boy, visiting the farm of some neighbor in the old Midwest of America. It wasn't even his own memory and was certainly far from the past of his isolated, mistrustful youth.

Out of some dark corner, movement. His father's consigliere Dominic Briggs manifested, surrounded by caviar and gold, and Fiske's throat tightened unexpectedly with confusion and pain, in that order. The pain ripened as his eyes ticked sideways to Carmine's portrait on the wall, and long-buried resentments raced anguish and regret from deep below into the light of day.

You! thought Fiske, staring at the portrait, alight with rage. *My life was a dark room, a bowl of promise removed, a malevolent plan in place. You!* he screamed in his mind, unhinged with a hatred that must have been there all his life. He was surprised by it, and not surprised. A strange buoyancy of unrestraint lightened his bones. *Not one ounce of genuine love! This is what you created!* his mind shouted exuberantly. *What do you think of me now?*

This was it. There would be no more. Fiske realized in a rush there would be no future. Not for him. It had all been for naught, all of it, he now knew, as he watched the earth rushing to meet him. And that was the moment when he pushed against the crushing table enough to gather the air into his lungs and scream. Except it was not a scream but a defiant bellow, directed at his father's portrait, tumescent with mutiny and grief, sixty-five years too late.

***

Lex steadied herself on the seat of the recliner, her feet sinking awkwardly into the plush material, and gripped the handhold tighter.

They had dragged the chair to one side of the hatch, and Rosewood stood on the other side peering into an open wall panel. He had strongly disagreed that Alexia should be the one to engage in assault but had relented, acknowledging her uncompromising (and disturbingly fierce) desire for vengeance.

He threw surreptitious glances at her, riding between the immense relief that his daughter was still alive and the recognition that the Alexia he'd last seen, although only a few weeks ago, was gone, and this new young woman stood before him, the same but… more. The thought that she might have already started evolving and he'd been too busy to notice tried to muscle in, but he pushed it aside. No doubt that was true, but he would deal with it later. He would be a better father. She had been returned to him, and he would grab that second chance and never let go.

He fiddled with the panel, reconfirming that he'd located the correct wire, as someone started to unlock the hatch.

"Dad! Now!" Lex hissed.

Rosewood faced the panel, plucked out a wire, and the cabin plunged into darkness.

The hatch swung open, hinges squeaking, and Lex swiped the pipe down savagely.

There was a clang and a thud, and Rosewood hurriedly reconnected the wire. The lights snapped back on, revealing Harry on the floor, rubbing his head and glaring at Lex.

"Harry!" She grinned, overjoyed. As Harry stared, she belatedly hid the handhold behind her back. As the strained silence continued, she tossed it to the floor and cringed.

*⁎⁎

The hangar boiled with pandemonium as panic-stricken staff fled in different directions, yelling instructions or shrieking in terror. The wind howled. Loose objects and papers skittered through the air and along the floor. Aerolites lifted off, evacuating amid explosions, nearly colliding in their haste.

Harry, Lex, and Rosewood reached a section with several para-jets on a rig. Harry swiftly strapped one on Lex as estate personnel flung themselves out of the hangar wearing their own. Lex boggled at the ongoing destruction. When Harry finished securing the pack, he pulled her to the edge of the hangar. Lex's eyes grew wide as she stared out at the racing clouds.

"Hey, let's think about this!" Lex yelled over the wind.

"No time."

Harry picked her up and she wrapped herself around him like a terrified kitten.

"W-wait, Harry—"

Staring into her eyes, Harry pried off her arms and legs one by one. Then with no preamble, he tossed her out.

Lex plowed through the clouds, rolling, flailing, and screaming at the top of her lungs. Her skirt started flapping above her waist, and she stopped screaming long enough to yank it down around her knees, mortified. The maneuvering thrusters snapped out and ignited, straightening her descent, and then she was touching down gently on the ground. She teetered but kept her balance and craned her head back, searching for her father.

In the hangar, fumbling with his own pack, Rosewood approached Harry thoughtfully and pumped his arm.

"I don't know where Alexia found you—or you found her—but I'm glad you did. Both of you."

Harry reached out and snapped one last clasp together on Rosewood's straps.

"Thank you, son."

Rosewood shot Harry a tense smile, turned, and stepped out of the hangar. Harry leaned over, following his descent into and below the clouds, then turned and stalked away with purpose.

***

Tapestries rained from the walls amidst bits of debris knocked loose from each successive explosion. Halfway down the stairway in the grand vestibule, Moss's clone stood rooted in place as a stream of hysterical staff stampeded past him. Still dressed in a light blue medical gown with bandages on his head and the neck brace in place, the clone rotated his entire body awkwardly, searching for an exit.

"How do I get out of here?" he asked no one in particular and then resumed picking his way down the rest of the stairs. At the bottom he turned right, paused, changed his mind, turned left and slammed into a wall.

Except it wasn't a wall.

It was Harry.

Reaching down to wrench the clone up from where he'd fallen, Harry bellowed, "Moss!"

His brain not even registering the blinding pain the collision had caused, the clone's eyes flew open wide, his entire body shuddering with alarm. Harry shook him once by the flimsy front of the gown, tearing the material, then roughly shoved him back. "Where's Colonel Moss?"

Sagging, the clone pointed upstairs with a trembling finger. As Harry turned and barreled away, Moss's clone stared after him in disbelief, cold terror setting in. He'd recognized the Master Link behind the man's ear. "Twenty-Seven," he muttered with bone deep dread, unable to look away from where Harry had disappeared. A loud boom blasted close by and shook the floor, dislodging part of the ceiling which came crashing down. Jostled from his trance by the explosion, he stumbled after a string of fleeing staff.

Winchester's rifle primed, Harry searched the sterile medical area methodically, kicking in one door after the other. He peered inside each and moved to the next.

A staffer popped out of a room clinging to a satchel stuffed with medical equipment, a blue, red, and green New Years hat still perched absurdly on his head. Not even noticing the gun, he shoulder-checked Harry as he sprinted past screaming, "It's going down—it's going down!"

As if to egg on his hysteria, another concussion sent rumbling waves through the walls and floors. The man rounded the corner at top speed and disappeared. Harry continued down the hall. The next kicked-in door revealed what looked like a recovery room, also empty, but the one after that, obviously an operating room, was still occupied.

A cloaked body lay unmoving on a surgical table.

Harry approached hesitantly, slung the Enforcer, and paused. Then he tore the sheet off and stilled, as Fiske's estate canted in the sky, unsure of what he was seeing.

Reaching forward, he plucked at the bandages wrapped around Moss's head and unraveled them, pulling lightly at the parts stuck together by blood and other unidentifiable fluids. As the bandages fluttered to the ground, Harry detected a thin line surrounding the corpse's skull. He leaned forward, gripped the top, and . . . pop. An empty brain casing stared back.

Harry straightened, feeling strange, as if someone had poured boiling tar onto his body. Indexed images flew through his mind, starting with the war on Mars and ending with the empty cavity of Moss's abandoned body, the yawning evidence of further craven deception.

Harry raced from the room.

CHAPTER 33

The hangar was deserted, except for Moss's clone struggling over the pitching floor toward the last para-jet.

The wind whistled. Loose objects and abandoned pieces of clothing and papers swirled around as the walls shook with each detonation. The clone absently kicked a blue, red, and green New Years hat which lifted into the air and was sucked out the open hangar.

Moss's clone fumbled with the para-jet, clumsily attaching the harness with his limited mobility, perspiring heavily. His head bandage had come undone and part of it was stuck to his face, plastered by sweat.

"Colonel Moss!"

The clone snapped up. Harry's rifle was trained between his eyes.

"You betrayed us!" Harry yelled over the thundering wind.

"Twenty-Seven!"

"You betrayed the unit!"

The clone stood rigidly, clinging to the para-jet's straps.

"What I did was save humanity from enslavement!"

Harry's aim wavered, his resolve suddenly uncertain. Lowering the rifle a millimeter, he stared at the clone, watching as he stealthily backed up toward the open hangar.

"I discovered Zim's plan. He used an unlimited military budget to try to subjugate the human race!" The clone's eyes ticked sideways to gauge how far he had to go. "I stopped him!"

Harry's face hardened, and he lifted the rifle.

"Father would never—"

"You've regained some of your memories. Reference file Operation Archangel!"

Harry's eyes immediately glossed over as he found and accessed the Archangel file . . . and something else.

"Zim was planning to use the Sentinels to dominate the human race." Moss's clone glanced behind him again. "You were merely an instrument in his diabolical scheme."

Still accessing, Harry stuttered, "But my brothers . . . you destroyed—"

"They're operational!"

Harry stopped accessing. His eyes found the clone. He stared, thunderstruck.

"Five self-destructed. Six and eighteen were destroyed in the explosion, but the others . . . the others are here, on Earth." The clone continued talking, continued slowly backing up. He pushed the plastered strand of bandage away from his eye to clear his peripheral vision. "Operational on condition that their memories be suppressed so that they could never threaten humanity's freedom."

"Where . . . "

"You'd need their link codes," the clone told him. "Zim took them to his grave."

Harry's turmoil gave way to hardness of purpose, and he raised the rifle once more.

"Colonel Moss, you're under arrest for treason."

Moss's clone had reached his goal, the edge of the hangar opening.

"Arrest? By you?" The clone threw his hands up. "Look around you!"

Sucking winds yanked at his hospital gown and further unraveled his head bandages. Another explosion had them both careening sideways, fighting for their footing.

"This is what you are! You're a weapon, a destroyer of worlds!"

Harry faltered once more, his focus submerged beneath a surge of conflicting thoughts, memories, and beliefs.

"History will call me a hero. My sacrifice has saved mankind from Zim's monsters. From you, Twenty-Seven!"

Moss's clone fell backward out of the hangar.

"COLONEL!" Harry bellowed.

Harry reeled, all sound fading, leaving only his circulation pump thumping as he yanked down his visor and studied a digital layout of the hangar, quickly locating a blinking light designated fire control.

Lifting the visor, Harry leapt clear across the expanse of the hangar and landed at English's station. After flipping several switches, the screens lit up. He locked onto Moss's clone tumbling through the air and assigned a missile. His finger hovered over the big red fire button but suddenly halted an inch above it. Lying on the console beside the button was Lex's skull and crossbones knapsack, and Harry found himself straying from the button to pick up the bag as Zim's long-buried voice reverberated through his core.

Remember, you are not killers.

Harry staggered back as if pushed by an invisible force. A tumult of voices emerged, cascading through integrated memory circuits, and Duesenberg's worried face flew out from the dark.

For compassion's sake, don't kill anybody else.

Lex followed, kneeling in the dirt in Undertown, staring up at him.

A Bodhisattva vows to take on the suffering of others and suffer instead.

"*Cause and effect,*" Jasper told him. "*What goes around comes around.*"

Harry's face slackened as he gripped the bag tightly.

Don't you feel any compassion?

I don't feel . . . anything.

The floor of the doomed estate began tilting inexorably at an impossible angle.

Alarms blared and somewhere nearby flames roared, slowly filling the hangar with black acrid smoke. Harry saw and heard none of it. His electronic pulse continued thumping, a steady rhythm behind the montage of memories flooding his mind.

Lex kneeled before the shrine beneath the black sky.

When you let go of your ego's attachments, you end suffering.

Her voice rang out from Jasper's destroyed garage: *Nobody should suffer from some old memory.*

Harry pulled the knapsack close, his thoughts wheeling.

You think Mechs go to heaven, Harry? Winchester's bass voice rumbled.

The alleyway from 43rd Street appeared before Harry's eyes, cold and inhospitable-looking in the murky afternoon light. It seemed as if it had been years ago, but it had only been yesterday. He saw the ascetic sitting there, watched as he pressed his hands together and bared a toothless smile. His words spun out into the air, brightly lit, golden, in Harry's mind, sparkling like gleaming gems, each syllable momentous, each word a revelation:

The compassionate heart has already attained heaven.

The sounds of mayhem and destruction rushed back with world-ending violence. Harry flipped backwards to the tilting deck and bolted for the para-jet rig.

It was empty.

The alarms shrilled, the flames roared, the black smoke swirled. A resounding boom jolted the room once again, dislodging an overhead pipe, which landed squarely on top of the red fire button.

"Missile away," the computer announced.

Harry stood still as stone as Jasper's voice licked at the edges of his consciousness: *"Trust in your karma, Harry."*

Smoke wound between Harry's legs and pressed against his face as all voices and recollection and feeling coalesced into an olio of refined fusion. It felt as if something deep inside, or from completely outside of himself, instantly transmuted, shifting reality almost imperceptibly, invisibly, yet irrevocably. An unfamiliar sensation, a strange *mindfulness*, coated his manufactured innards and unmanufactured essence with egalitarian intent.

The para-jets were all gone. The aerolites had all taken off. As Harry fought for balance in the collapsing estate, he experienced an odd serenity when he realized that there was no way to escape and, more surprisingly, that it was all right.

And then he remembered something.

CHAPTER 34

His gown snapping in the wind, mooning the birds and the sky alike, the clone watched the ground coming up fast.

A sense of victory swelled, flushing the new skin of his new face, pumping fresh blood through his brand-new heart. He gazed out over Empire City with 20/20 vision, all the familiar aches and pains gone, and it seemed like the day was dawning for him alone.

He inhaled and exhaled a long, gratified breath . . . as something darted between the clouds in his peripheral vision.

The clone twisted, right, then left, searching. He had seen something. Had he seen something? But now there was nothing, save the rushing air, and just as he was about to relax again, a rocket roared above him.

He gasped, terrified.

There was a rocket. Stalking him. A rocket was stalking him. He couldn't think straight. Suddenly, an urgent beeping issued from his para-jet. Maneuvering thrusters snapped out and fired to straighten out his descent.

"No, no, no, NO, NO, NOOOOOOOOO!"

The retro rocket ignited as the missile made a wide arc, racing toward the sudden heat source. In midair, clone and missile became one in a fireball.

***

Moss's clone exploded while Lex was still searching for her father. It seemed like a long time since she'd landed, and she'd thought he was right behind her. Straining to see past the other wanderers, she finally spotted him in the distance, turning in a slow circle, obviously searching for her too. She glanced up at the fireball then jogged awkwardly his way but stopped as the para-jet thumped heavily on her back. She snapped off the harness and let the gear drop. The booming sound of the falling estate thundered through the clouds as she power-walked toward her father who was now also heading in her direction.

All around them, the Atlantic wasteland was populated with those who had jumped ship. They picked their way numbly over the uneven Atlantic coastal shelf. Barren and bald, it was strewn with the trash and objects that had fallen out of the hangar door. Lex and her father stumbled toward each other and fell into each other's arms.

Finally letting go of her father, Lex rotated in a circle, scanning the area as far as she could see.

As the massive property plummeted the last couple hundred meters, they backpedaled a few steps even though the crash site was miles and miles away. It nosedived into the ground then snapped in half, skipped once, and exploded. The ground bucked. The firestorm and sudden wind pushed like a giant invisible hand against Lex and her father. The fire dimmed quickly, the howling wind fading to a murmur.

"No . . . " Lex tripped over an unseen object. Her father caught her by the arm. "No. . . "

***

The two of them drifted like specters amidst the twisted, burning Dantean landscape. Above them, emergency aerolites extinguished fires while others began picking up survivors. Wreckage from the mansion had been flung everywhere—smashed computer terminals, pots and paintings, parts of beds, starched white uniforms still somehow looking freshly laundered. Half a staircase stood upright, leading to nowhere. What looked like the remains of a massive marble table had slid through the dirt, shoving up mounds of earth before stopping.

Lex trudged forward, her skin layered with grit, beyond exhausted.

"Alexia." Rosewood stopped walking and faced his daughter. "No one could have survived this."

Lex gazed out at the devastation.

"Harry could," she said.

With that, she began picking her way forward again, scrutinizing every lump and bulge and unidentifiable object that lay before them.

A rhythmic thudding brought her to a halt. Energized, Lex threw her head back, searching the sky for the next crashing disaster. Rosewood moved beside her, tilting his head back too.

The thudding continued. Lex and Rosewood turned completely around.

Behind them, half buried under fragments of wood, shattered plaster and chunks of concrete, was Moss's armored container lying on one side.

Lex grabbed her father's arm.

As they watched, the hatch on the container yawned open, creaking wildly, then slammed against the side with a loud crash. A hand emerged, feeling for purchase on the rim, then another hand followed. Then Harry pulled himself up. He positioned himself on the edge of the cabin, looking satisfied, legs dangling, as Rosewood gaped and Lex's hands flew brashly to her hips.

"Where have *you* been?"

Harry reached behind him and pulled up her knapsack.

"You forgot your bag."

Lex's face lit up, her mouth stretching into a dazzling, exuberant smile that melted into heartfelt affection and no small amount of wonder when she realized that Harry was smiling back.

CHAPTER 35

For now the world keeps turning and I keep breathing, in and out, in and out. I breathe in the life that is all around me, in this garden, in this city, in the fields beyond it, in the seas beyond them and the shores on the other side; life that reaches out towards the unreachable, unknowable space that is beyond all of us and the stars that burn there.
–The Year of the Rat, Claire Furniss

New Years celebrations were in full swing in Empire City and Times Square was nearly at a standstill. The Jumbotrons featured animations of a rat bouncing along replayed on a loop accompanied by digital fireworks and Happy New Year 2140 scrolling across in alternating gold and silver letters.

A drumline marching behind performers wearing happy Buddha masks produced a wall of thundering percussion as Dragon dancers bounded to the rhythmic beat. Random fireworks still whistled here and there, adults and children alike gripped New Year Rat balloons and red paper lanterns dotted the sky.

Harry, Lex, Dr. Rosewood, Jasper, Cecil and Duesenberg crowded around a food vendor where Lex stood stuffing her face. Behind the metallic counter, Chef Ghislaine Robuchon, swathed in a lumpy wool coat and unisex earflap hat, deftly maneuvered soydogs, sweet brioche buns, and condiments with the air of a seasoned veteran. Which she was. The only difference being a moveable feast of soydog rollers and bun steamers versus gleaming floors and expansive food prep spaces.

Chef Robuchon was pleased with the girl's appetite, convinced it could be nothing less due to the special spices she added to her product that none of the other vendors bothered with, as far as she could tell. And this was only the beginning. Soydog rollers now. Sous vide immersion circulators very soon.

Cecil leaned toward Lex. "You might wanna slow down," he suggested.

"Get-away-from-the-food," Lex said around a half-torn-apart soydog drowning in mustard that had dripped a yellow line down her blazer.

Cecil recoiled.

Chef Robuchon looked on, pleased, having no idea the young girl hadn't eaten in almost twenty-four hours. It had been an amazing day for the chef. Not only had an old friend who'd gotten into the mobile food business years ago immediately rented her a cart, but she'd evidently jumped ship just in time, too, considering that the Fiske estate was now enmeshed within the barren Atlantic shelf. She could still see rescue vehicles miles away over the area of the crash. The sterling tea set she had pilfered, along with Fiske's favorite solid gold salt and pepper shakers, had rented her a room *and* this cart, and she was already making profits. In high spirits, her mind swam with future plans and dreams.

The Hanna hat cabbie from yesterday stuck his head out of his cab's window impatiently.

"Yo, *today*. To-day!"

Rosewood began to bag Lex's food, but she kept grabbing it back and shoving it into her mouth as the chef smirked in the background and turned to new customers flocking to her cart.

"Alexia, we'll be late for the train."

"Okay!" She huffed, swallowing loudly. She turned to Jasper and Duesenberg who were quietly conferring as they gazed out at the mini-parades and dancing throngs. Harry stood silently beside them, single-mindedly watching his client, the girl in the battered school uniform.

"Thank you for everything." She smiled at Jasper and Duesenberg. "Thank you for helping Harry."

"Our pleasure, young lady," said Jasper.

"Best of luck," Duesenberg bowed his head slightly, fingering his bow tie.

Lex turned to Cecil. He'd extended his legs and towered over them, people watching. With a click and a whir, he compressed them, dropping down to normal height. He threw his arms open wide for a hug. "Bring it in," he said with his chrome-toothed grin.

"Yeah, right," said Lex. Instead, she gripped one of his hands and pumped it vigorously, causing wavy loops in his flexible arm. Cecil frowned in disappointment.

Rosewood pulled his daughter against him as he faced Harry. "If you desire, I can transplant your brain into a clone. As a thank you. For protecting the most precious thing in my life."

Harry considered the offer as everyone stared, waiting for his response.

If someone had told him ahead of time what would transpire in the past twenty-four hours, he would have pegged them for delusional at the least, a grifter at the most. But as the new year unfolded before him, awash in color and sound, the immensity of his discoveries struck him anew. The veil had been torn not only off his past but also his psyche, as it were, expanding limited vistas into never-before-felt or understood awareness.

It was as if he'd gone from two dimensions to three overnight, and he'd never felt so utterly light and free.

"I know what I was designed to be," Harry told Lex's father. "I need to discover what I'm capable of becoming."

Rosewood rested a fatherly hand on Harry's shoulder.

"A noble pursuit, son."

Pulling away from her father, Lex threw herself at Harry and hugged him, hard. "I'll never forget you," she whispered. Harry returned the embrace.

She let go and felt around in her knapsack. Removing the Forever-Rose, she crooked her finger at him. Harry leaned down and she handed him the rose. Getting on her toes, she said in his ear, "Hard Luck Harry's just another name for bodhisattva." She kissed him on the cheek and turned to leave.

Harry touched his cheek, gaze pinned on Lex and her father as they got into the cab. She pressed her face against the window and waved as the cab powered up, lifted off, and merged with the busy traffic above.

Cecil and Jasper waved back.

"Now I seen it all," said Jasper.

He picked up several shopping bags from the sidewalk. "A weapon of mass destruction disarmed by a kiss." He walked with Cecil to the curb where Cecil's scooter was parked. "Ain't that a kick in the pants? C'mon, Cecil, let's go fix Leonard."

Jasper climbed on the scooter behind Cecil looking miserable. As they rolled off into the chaos, Jasper's voice trailed back unhappily, "How humiliating."

"Later, action dude!" Cecil called excitedly.

"Slow down!"

"If I go any slower, we might as well walk!"

"Cut the back talk, Cecil!"

They disappeared into the crowd. Duesenberg sighed.

"Well, Harry, with the Boss of Empire City a pile of ashes, know what happens next?"

Harry frowned slightly. "No."

"A hostile takeover, of course."

Duesenberg braced against the cold, eyed Harry gloomily, and trudged away. "There's an ancient curse, 'May you live in interesting times.' Well, things are about to get real interesting around here." He walked a few more feet and called, "Happy New Year, pal!"

The 8-bit Star Spangled Banner notes sprang from Harry's PDA, and he pulled it free and read it. He tucked the Forever-Rose inside his duster, lowered his visor and rushed into the crush of bodies thinking, *I'm not unique, and I'm not alone. My brothers are out there, and I'm gonna find 'em.*

As Harry was swallowed into the crowd of jam-packed revelers, the laughter, the chatter, the dancing, the singing, the joy, despite the toil, despite the pain, of being alive, the clouds broke apart above the giant Buddha and a ray of sunlight briefly kissed its golden face.

I'm Harry. It's New Year's Day, Year of the Rat, my birthday.

ABOUT THE AUTHOR

F.A. Corporan grew up in Brooklyn and studied at the School of Visual Arts in New York. His writing has placed as finalist in both Emerging Writers and Unique Voices for Diverse Writers. Now residing in LA, he writes speculative and science fiction when not mountain biking, beta testing video games, and enjoying street photography.

S.E Bryan is a San Francisco born, LA-based author who has worked in Wyoming, lived in New York, hiked to the bottom of the Grand Canyon, and summited Mt. Whitney, the tallest mountain in the lower forty-eight. A lover of speculative fiction, Bryan enjoys creating worlds with brash characters in unexpected and humorous situations.